a purse
full of tales

Published by Hesperus Press Limited
28 Mortimer Street, London W1W 7RD
www.hesperuspress.com

A Purse Full of Tales first published by
Hesperus Press Limited, 2019.

Copyright © Chan Young Kim and David Carter, 2019

The right of Chan Young Kim and David Carter to be identified
as the Authors of the Works has been asserted by them in
accordance with Copyright, Designs and Patents Act 1988

Illustrations © John Shelley
Design by Madeline Meckiffe
Printed by Liber Duplex Barcelona

ISBN: 978-1-84391-653-6

All rights reserved. This book is sold subject
to the condition that it shall not be resold, lent,
hired out or otherwise circulated without the
express prior consent of the publisher.

a purse full of tales

folk tales from korea

retold by
chan young kim
and david carter

with illustrations by
john shelley

contents

preface

a purse full of tales

the woodcutter and the heavenly maiden

the sun and the moon

the disobedient tree frog

the lazy man who became an ox

a poor father's legacies

the grateful magpies

the golden axe and the silver axe

the spring of youth

rose and lotus

the fly and the sparrow

the good brother
and the bad brother

how the hare escaped from the tiger

the forgetful *dokkaebi*

the good girl and her stepsister

a bride for one grain of millet

the serpent bridegroom

from corn cakes to riches

the cat in a palanquin

the mud snail lady

why the sea is salty

preface

This book is not written for academic readers, but for ordinary readers – the children and the adults who still have a child in their spirit. Some of the stories were originally myths, legends and ancient novels, as well as folk tales. But all of them have been passed down from mouth to mouth, from generation to generation, over the ages. And one of the present storytellers, Chan Young Kim, heard most of the stories from his parents or on the radio, and read them in books, in his childhood.

These stories originated in different regions of North and South Korea. But we did not separate them into different geographical sections as they have been told throughout the two countries, before and after the division, transcending ideological barriers. Readers, however, will be able to recognise occasionally, through some phrasing, whether a story is from the north or the south part of the Korean Peninsula.

Korean folk tales include many supernatural and surrealistic elements, as do those from other civilisations. These elements are mainly based on such traditional religions as Shamanism, Buddhism and Taoism. We feel the need briefly to explain some of them, in order to help the reader develop a better insight into the stories.

1) Spirits: according to the animistic elements of Shamanism, Koreans have believed that all animals, plants and non-living objects have a spirit.

2) Ghosts: when a person has died with an unresolved resentment, they become a ghost and wander around in this world instead of going on to the next world. Occasionally the terms 'ghosts' and 'spirits' are used interchangeably.

3) The next world: death is not the end of existence. A person makes a journey on to the next world and continues to live there. This is different from the Buddhist concept of reincarnation. The Shamanist next world is another space where people continue to live, usually as they did in this world.

4) Heaven: above this world there is a space inhabited by divine beings. Occasionally 'heaven' and 'the skies' are referred to, meaning the same thing.

5) The heavenly god: in the traditional pantheistic cosmology, this god is the most omnipotent.

Apart from these, mythical creatures called *dokkaebis* appear quite frequently in Korean folk tales. They are of human size, generally looking like humans, usually with a horn on their heads and much hair on their bodies. They can be frightening, but also humorous and witty. Despite their mischievous behaviour, they also help good-natured people who are in distress and punish vicious people.

Tigers are other important creatures in Korean folk tales. Strong and frightening, they are often used as the symbol of people in a privileged social status. The animal, however, is usually depicted as stupid and pathetic. Quite often it ends up being tricked or trapped. Through this kind of representation, ordinary people have projected their wishes for revenge onto their oppressors.

Through a considerable number of stories the readers will find that certain virtues, such as generosity and compassion, are encouraged while greed and meanness are discouraged. But these aspects, together with the religious elements, are not imposed on the readers as in a sermon. Instead they are blended well into the interesting situation of each story with wit, humour and jests of various kinds.

a purse full of tales

Once upon a time there lived a boy who liked to listen to stories. He loved them even more than eating delicious food. But he would not tell a single one of the stories to others. Instead he wrote down each story on a piece of paper, folded it up small and put it in his purse. Then he tied the neck of the purse tightly to keep the stories to himself.

After several years the purse became crammed with stories. Confined within the purse, the stories could hardly move, although it was their nature to circulate freely. Eventually many of them died of suffocation and became spirits.

When the boy came of age, he was to be married to a young lady who lived in a village over the hills. On the eve of the wedding many of his relatives and their servants were staying in his house. So one of his servants had to sleep in a corner of his room. This servant was to lead the bridegroom on his horse to the bride's house. According to the custom in those days, the wedding usually took place in the courtyard of the bride's house.

Soon after dinner the bridegroom fell asleep, and so did the servant. In the middle of night, however, the servant was disturbed by some sounds: there was whispering in the room. Pricking up his ears, he could hear talking from inside the purse, which was fastened to the bridegroom's waist.

A voice said: 'This bastard is still keeping stories cooped up in this purse. It's time he was punished.'

Another voice said: 'Tomorrow he'll go to the bride's house for the wedding. Let's get him on his way there.'

But how should they do it?

One voice suggested: 'It's a long procession to the bride's house. He'll feel thirsty on the journey. So I'll be a tempting pear on a tree, and if he eats me, he will die.'

Another voice said: 'In case he doesn't eat the pear, I'll be some water in a clear spring. If he drinks me, he will die.'

A third voice said: 'If this bastard doesn't drink the water either, I'll be a cushion full of needles. When he sits on me in the wedding marquee, he will die.'

Having heard these words, the servant resolved firmly to use all means possible to protect the bridegroom against the story spirits. The next morning, however, the bridegroom's father unexpectedly said to the servant: 'We need to change our plans a little. I want you to stay here and look after guests. Another servant will lead the procession.'

'But I must go with young master, sir.'

'How dare you! Are you disobeying your master?'

The servant insisted vehemently on leading the bridegroom's horse. He said he would rather die than stay in the house. So the master allowed him to lead the bridegroom's horse at the head of the procession.

Halfway through the journey the bridegroom started to feel thirsty. When he saw a juicy-looking pear on a tree along the path, he wanted to eat it. But the servant refused to stop and pick the fruit. 'No, young master,' he said. 'A wild pear would be bad for you.' And he pulled on the reins of the horse to make it move on quickly.

When the procession approached the top of a hill, a spring of clear water came into view. A dipper, made from a gourd, was floating on the water. The bridegroom was feeling really parched and was desperate to have some of the water. So he ordered the servant: 'Stop here. And bring me a dipper of water from the spring.'

But the servant pretended not to have heard the order. He urged the horse up to the hilltop. When the young master became angry, the servant just said: 'We'll be late for the wedding.'

The bridegroom and the rest of the procession arrived safely at the bride's house. They entered the wedding marquee. The bridegroom went towards his seat. As he was just about to sit down, the servant suddenly lifted him in his arms and placed him on another chair. The servant had caught sight of the points of some needles in the cushion on the bridegroom's seat.

Being unaware of this, the bridegroom was burning with anger. He felt he was being embarrassed in public by the servant. He decided he would punish the servant severely as soon as they arrived back home. The servant had behaved very rudely and strangely!

Later, when the servant heard about the bridegroom's complaints and his intention to punish him, he explained about the story spirits. Now the bridegroom understood the whole situation. He thanked the servant, and loosened the neck of his purse so that the stories escaped and were able to travel around freely.

the woodcutter and the heavenly maiden

A long, long time ago, when tigers also smoked, a young woodcutter lived at the foot of the Diamond Mountains, together with his elderly mother. He collected firewood in the mountains every day to buy food for his mother and himself. He was an honest man and he worked hard. But no women wanted to marry him as he was so poor.

One day, while the woodcutter was chopping wood, a roe deer staggered towards him. The deer had an arrow stuck in his hind leg. It pleaded to the woodcutter, terrified: 'Please hide me! Save my life!!' The woodcutter quickly hid the deer in the pile of firewood he had collected. Shortly after that a hunter came running over to the woodcutter, with a bow and arrow in his hand.

'Hey there, have you seen a deer running this way? I'm chasing it.' said the hunter, panting.

'Yes, I did see one. It was running down there,' replied the hunter, pointing in the direction of a valley. The hunter set off immediately in that direction.

As soon as the hunter had gone away, the deer came out of the woodpile.

'Phew, you've saved my life! I'd like to show my gratitude to you.'

The woodcutter just stood there silently.

'I'm going to tell you something, and if you do as I tell you, you will have good fortune.'

The deer told the woodcutter that some heavenly maidens would come down to visit the earth. And the deer also advised him what he should do and should not do on that occasion. Then, as soon as the woodcutter had pulled the arrow from his leg and bound up the wound with his sash, the deer ran off.

On the fifteenth night of the month, when the moon was full, the woodcutter went into the Diamond Mountains, as the deer had told him to. Indeed, there was a clear and beautiful lake between two peaks. The woodcutter hid himself behind a rock, near the lake,

and waited. Soon, when the moon reached its highest point, three heavenly maidens flew down onto the shore, in gracefully fluttering dresses.

They chatted merrily while taking off their clothes and hanging them on the big pine trees nearby. Then they plunged into the water, where they bathed happily and playfully for quite a long while.

The woodcutter remembered what the deer had told him and crept towards the pine trees. He removed the dress of the youngest heavenly maiden, went back and hid it behind the rock.

Towards daybreak the heavenly maidens hurried out of the water. They started to put on their clothes, except the youngest one. To her astonishment her dress was missing.

'What happened to my dress? It's gone.'

She started to search around, with the help of the other two. But they could not find it.

'Oh, it's time we were back in heaven,' said one of the others.

'I hope you'll find it soon. Don't be back too late,' said the other.

Then they flew off into the air.

The woodcutter went close to the heavenly maiden, who had crouched down, sobbing.

'What's the matter?' he asked, pretending not to understand. As the heavenly maiden didn't reply, he suggested: 'You can come to my house and stay there, if you like . . .'

There was nothing else the heavenly maiden could do but follow him to his house. And so she started to live there with the woodcutter and his elderly mother. With the help of the kind woodcutter she gradually learned to adapt herself to life on the earth.

Eventually they got married. The woodcutter collected firewood even more diligently, and the heavenly maiden cooked, washed and cleaned the house for their family. The three of them were really happy.

One problem, however, was that the heavenly maiden missed her family and friends in heaven. Sometimes her nostalgia overwhelmed her. The woodcutter felt guilty and sympathetic about it. He wanted to confess what he had done and plead for her forgiveness. But he couldn't . . . He remembered vividly what the roe deer had told him. So he had to wait longer until the time was right.

The next year the heavenly maiden gave birth to a boy. But she still missed heaven occasionally.

Fortunately, after having a second son, she seemed to settle down completely into life on the earth. The woodcutter decided to tell her the truth about her heavenly dress, although the deer had told him to wait until they had three children.

The woodcutter pulled the dress from the bottom of a cabinet. He had removed it from behind the rock and hidden it there. As soon as the heavenly maiden saw the dress, she put it on. Then she regained her magical powers, and immediately she flew away back to heaven, with one of her children in each arm.

Since the heavenly maiden and the children had left him, the woodcutter was heartbroken and could neither eat nor sleep for several days. Then an idea struck him: he might have a chance to see the deer again. So, every day he climbed up to the place where he had met the deer. While collecting wood in an absent-minded way, he paid close attention to the sounds around him. And, after several days, the same deer came by again.

'I need your help,' said the woodcutter honestly, blocking the deer's way. 'The heavenly maiden has returned to heaven, taking the children with her. What should I do?'

The deer said: 'Since the heavenly maidens had the problem that night, they don't come down to bathe any more.' It paused for a while, and then continued: 'There's one way, though. Now they draw water from the lake by lowering a bucket all the way down from heaven with a rope. Fortunately you can go up there in the bucket.'

So several days later the woodcutter went to the lake and waited, as the deer had told him to. At midnight a large bucket came down from heaven to the water. Without hesitation the woodcutter got into the bucket and held the rope firmly with his hands. Then the bucket started to go up again.

When he arrived in heaven, he was crouching down in the bucket to conceal himself. But the heavenly maidens could sense him by his smell.

'I can smell a man from the earth,' one of them said, and discovered the woodcutter in the bucket.

'What are you doing here?' asked she, astounded.

The woodcutter told the heavenly maidens why he had come there. They took him to the King of Heaven to let him judge. There he met his children and his wife, who turned out to be a daughter of the heavenly king!

The King of Heaven allowed the woodcutter to stay in the heavenly kingdom. Together with the heavenly princess and their children, the woodcutter started to live happily again. He enjoyed all kinds of delicious food, wore beautiful silk clothes and had no cares and worries.

One day, however, the woodcutter suddenly thought of his old mother, whom he had left alone on the earth. He wanted to go and see if she was well. But his wife, the heavenly princess, did not want him to go and visit his mother. She worried that he might not come back to heaven.

The woodcutter was so concerned about his mother that he became ill. As the days passed, his illness worsened. Eventually the heavenly princess agreed to let him visit his mother, with some conditions: 'You will go down to the earth on this flying horse. Pay a brief visit to your mother. But don't ever dismount the horse. Once you touch the ground, you won't be able to return here.'

As soon as the woodcutter mounted the flying horse, it flew down to the earth in the twinkling of an eye.

When his mother saw him in the courtyard on the horse's back, she was overjoyed.

'Where have you been?' she said. 'I thought you were dead or something.' And she urged him to come into the house. But he explained briefly that he could not stay long and had to leave soon.

'Well, then, why don't you have some pumpkin porridge before you leave? I made the dish every day while you were away.'

Pumpkin porridge was the woodcutter's favourite food. He did not dare to disappoint his mother as he did not know when he would be able to see her again. So, he sat astride the flying horse and took a bowl of pumpkin porridge from her. But the bowl was so hot that he dropped it on the horse's back. And, startled by the hot porridge, the horse flung him off and flew back to heaven.

From that day the woodcutter started to miss his wife and children in heaven very much. He missed them so much that he just stood in tears in the courtyard and looked up at the sky all day. There was no way he could return to heaven, so instead he wanted to be as near there as possible. And . . . when he died of grief, he became a cockerel.

From early morning, every day, the cockerel flew up to the highest point of the roof of the house. There it crowed with its neck stretched up towards heaven. And it is still doing it till this day.

the sun and the moon

A long, long time ago there was a woman who lived deep in the mountains, together with her young son and daughter. She was a poor single mother, so she had to make a living all by herself. She did all sorts of odd jobs for wealthy families in neighbouring villages.

One day she had to go to work on a farm far away beyond the hills. As she was leaving home, she warned her children firmly: 'Don't open the door to anyone except me. Feel the person's hand first, and open the door only when you're sure it's mine.'

On the farm she worked very hard. And for this the farm owner gave her some rice cakes for her children. When it was near dinner time, she hurried off home, thinking of her children left there all alone.

Soon it started to get dark. And as she was about to go over the first hill, a tiger appeared out of the woods. He blocked her way, and, opening his great red mouth, said: 'My dear lady, if you give me a rice cake, I won't eat you up.'

She quickly put a rice cake into the tiger's open mouth. The tiger promptly disappeared back into the woods.

When the mother was hurrying over the second hill, the tiger turned up again. Blocking the path, he said:

'My dear lady, if you give me a rice cake, I won't eat you up.' And every time the mother was going over a hill, the tiger appeared and demanded another rice cake.

To her relief, she finally reached the top of the hill which was the nearest to her home. When the tiger demanded a rice cake again, however, she could not offer one. So she told him honestly: 'I've run out of them. You ate them all.'

'In that case, I'll eat you up.'

The tiger promptly pounced on the mother and gobbled her up. And then he put her handkerchief on his head and set out for her house, where the children were looking forward to her return.

When the tiger reached the house, he stood at the door and said: 'Children, children, Mummy's back. Open the door.'

The brother noticed that the voice sounded rather hoarse. He remembered what his mother had said to them as she left home in the morning. So he shouted out: 'Push your hand through the door!'

Immediately, tearing a hole in the paper screen door, the tiger thrust his front paw into the room. Even though the room was dark, the children could see that it was covered with bristles.

'This isn't Mummy's hand. Her hands are soft and smooth,' said the sister.

The tiger explained: 'My dear, today Mummy's been working very hard. It made her hands very rough.'

But the children would not open the door.

Suddenly the tiger had a good idea. He went into the kitchen, which was outside next to the room, and found

a bag of wheat flour. He put some on his front paws and went back to the door.

The tiger pushed his right front paw through the hole in the door again, and said: 'Look, my dear children, I've washed my hands.' And indeed, the paw looked soft and felt smooth.

The brother opened the iron door latch. And . . . the door was yanked open from outside. A big person was entering, with a handkerchief on his head. It wasn't their mother. It was a tiger!

The brother grabbed his younger sister by the wrist and ran out of the back door. He tried to find a place to hide. He saw the big tree in the backyard, which overlooked the well. They climbed the tree, hid themselves in it and held their breath.

The tiger started to search eagerly for the children in the backyard. He looked down into the well. There he saw a reflection of the children in the tree.

'Hey, children, how did you get up there?' asked the tiger, looking up at the tree.

The children didn't reply.

This time the tiger spoke in a kind, flattering voice: 'You're very clever! I really wonder how you managed to get there.'

The brother said: 'Fetch some sesame oil. Put it on the bark. Then, you can climb up easily.'

The stupid tiger went to the kitchen, found a bottle of sesame oil, and smeared it on the tree trunk. Each time he tried to climb the tree, he immediately slipped down onto his backside. And it hurt.

The children were amused by the tiger's behaviour

and chuckled. The tiger was angry, very angry. But he managed to control himself because he suddenly had a good idea. He stood up and, looking up at the tree, said in a caring voice: 'Oh, dear! How dangerous it is! You might fall down into the well and get drowned.'

Still, there was no response from the children. The tiger went on: 'Let me come up and help you down. So, tell me how can I get up there.'

'Use an axe. Chop footholds in the trunk,' the younger sister said abruptly, out of fear that they would fall into the well.

Soon the tiger brought an axe and started to climb up the tree by making footholds in it. Nearer and nearer he came up to the children. Full of fear, the children prayed to the heavens to be saved.

At any moment the tiger could stretch his paw, with its sharp claws, to grab one of the children. Then, however, a rope came down to them from the heavens. They grasped hold of it, and very soon they were pulled up.

The tiger did the same as the children. He prayed to the heavens. Then a rope came down from above. He held it firmly with his paws. The rope was lifted up, up and away! But high up in the air it suddenly broke. It was a rotten rope.

So, the tiger fell all the way down onto a sorghum plant, which pricked his backside.

Meanwhile, in the kingdom of heaven the brother and the sister lived happily for many days. Then, one day, the King of Heaven said to them: 'I don't want you to idle away your time here. Do something, for the people below, in the earthly world!'

He ordered the children to make the world brighter, by day and night. The younger sister insisted on becoming the sun because she was afraid of the night. So the brother had to become the moon.

As the sky became brighter, people looked up more often. It made the sister shy, so she started to shine more and more brightly, until it became impossible for people to look up at her. And that's why the sun is much brighter than the moon.

the disobedient tree frog

Once upon a time a young tree frog lived with his widowed mother by a small pond. He was very naughty and disobedient. He never listened to his mother, and he always did the opposite to what she told him to.

If his mother told him to play in the hills, he went down to the stream. If she said, 'Go east', he went west. If she told him to do this, he did that.

The mother worried a lot about her son's behaviour. 'What am I going to do with the boy?' she wondered. 'Other children behave very well. They respect their parents and don't cause them any trouble. But . . .' she sighed. 'Why can't my boy behave like them? I'm really worried what will become of him.'

The mother resolved to make him mend his ways. So, she called him to her and talked about it. The young frog, however, rejected her concern, saying: 'You don't have to worry about it at all. I'll be fine just the way I am now.'

'But you don't even croak properly. So, let's start with that. Now, repeat after me: "Croak".'

'Cork.'

The young frog said it back to front.

'No, no. C-R-O-A-K.'

'C-O-R-K.'

'Oh, really . . . !'

'Hee-hee! I told you not to worry.'

He laughed and hopped away.

Every day, the mother frog tried to teach the young frog how to behave properly. But he continued to ignore her. Her frustration grew day by day, week by week and month by month. Eventually she became ill and there was no hope for her to live much longer.

When she realised this, she called her son to her bedside and said: 'I don't think I can live much longer. When I die, don't bury me on the hillside. I want to be buried by the stream.' The mother frog actually wanted to be buried on a sunny hillside, as people usually were. But she said it in this way because she knew very well that her son would do the opposite.

A few days later the mother frog died. The young frog was very sad. He cried and cried bitterly: 'I always did the opposite to what she said, because it was fun. I didn't know it would cause her so much stress. Oh, she died because of me. What am I going to do now?'

From then on, the young tree frog decided to behave the way his mother had told him to. First, he buried his mother by the stream.

Soon the rainy season came, and it started to rain heavily. The stream rose higher and higher, and eventually it overflowed its banks. The young frog worried that his mother's grave would be washed away. So he went down to the stream, only to find that everything was sinking except a tall willow tree near the grave.

The young frog climbed the tree and kept watching his mother's grave. Little by little it was being washed away. Helplessly, he cried: 'Croak!' As more and more of the grave mound was washed away, he could not stop crying: 'Croak, croak, croak . . .'

Since then, whenever it was likely to rain, he climbed the tree and cried. That is why, when it rains, tree frogs climb a tree and cry sadly.

the lazy man
who became an ox

Once there was a lazy man who hated working. He hated it so much that he would rather die. Until well into his thirties he had never lifted a finger to do anything. Even when he got married, he did not change one little bit.

One summer it was extraordinarily hot and dry. There had been no rain for such a long time that people worried about their harvest. Their crops could be completely destroyed unless they were watered generously. So, people in the village agreed to dig a well.

The next day all the village people gathered together and worked hard on digging the well, but the lazy man stayed at home, napping all day. Embarrassed by his shameful behaviour, his wife nagged him as soon as she returned home from working with the others. The lazy man thought he could live more pleasantly if he got away from his wife. Then he would be able to idle away his days without being disturbed by anyone.

Early next morning he left home. He just walked and walked along a mountain path with no special destination in mind. After a while, however, he spotted a hut in the mountains. And in the yard an old man was squatting down on an ox fur and carving an ox head out of a piece of wood. The lazy man became curious about it. So he went to the old man and asked: 'What is the carving for, if I may ask?'

The old man looked up at him, smiled faintly and said: 'This brings good fortune to people . . . especially to those who don't like working.'

The lazy man opened his eyes wide, and in excitement he asked: 'Really? How?'

'It's hollow inside. If you put it on your head, all kinds of good things happen to you,' said the old man, looking into the lazy man's face.

'Can I try it on?' the lazy man asked boldly.

'No, sorry. This is for someone else,' said the old man, still looking into the lazy man's face.

The lazy man begged desperately for the old man to allow him to wear it, even for a short time. 'All right then. If you want to so much.'

The old man stood up with the wooden carving in his hands, and then put it on the lazy man's head. Immediately, the old man picked up the ox fur from the ground and put it on the lazy man's body. The lazy man's body became bent and his hands touched the ground.

The lazy man felt his body growing rapidly bigger. He wanted to take off the carving from his head and the fur coat from his body. But they were tightly stuck to him. 'What's happening to my body?' he shouted anxiously. But the words came out as 'Moo, moo, moo! Moo, moo!' He had turned into an ox.

Straightaway the old man put a ring into the ox's nose and fixed a rope on the ring. He led him out of the yard and all the way along a mountain path. When the rope

was pulled, it was so painful to his nose that he had to follow the old man helplessly.

At sunset they arrived at a cattle market. A farmer showed great interest in the ox.

'I need a working ox. Does your ox work hard?' asked the farmer.

'Yes, indeed,' replied the old man. 'He's very strong and works very hard,' and he added that the ox did not need feeding much.

Satisfied with what the old man said, the farmer decided to buy the ox. And as he was making the payment, the old man said slowly and clearly: 'Don't ever feed him turnips. They are not good for him and could kill him.'

The farmer thought that the old man was exaggerating and did not take him seriously. In a happy mood he returned home with the new ox he had just bought.

From then on, the ox had to work hard from dawn to late at night every day. He had to plough the hard soil of the vegetable gardens and harrow the muddy rice paddies. He had to carry heavy loads on his back, as well as turning a millstone. And all that he ate was dried rice straw.

When he crouched down in the smelly cowshed at night, he regretted deeply his laziness in the past. He wanted to become a man again. But how? Whenever he appealed to the farmer that he was not an ox, but a man, his voice just made the sound, 'Moo, moo'. Then the farmer whipped him on, usually saying: 'Gee up, gee up! What's the matter with this ox? There are lots of things to do today. Gee up, gee up!'

Finally, the lazy man decided that he would rather die than live as an ox. He remembered the warning the old man had given to the farmer in the cattle market. And he waited for a chance to eat a turnip.

Before long he found a good opportunity. Several days later he was led to a field with a turnip patch nearby. While ploughing the field, he was very attentive all the time to the farmer's movements. At mid-morning the farmer removed the ploughshare from him and went off the field to relieve himself.

The ox ran for his life. On reaching the turnip patch,

he ate a turnip hurriedly and waited for death. He did not die. Instead, he started to feel itchy all over his body.

When the farmer returned to his field, he screamed with fear. His ox had disappeared and in its place was standing a young man.

The young man explained to the farmer what had happened to him. He said goodbye to the farmer and immediately left.

On his way back home he began to wonder about the old man in the mountain hut. When he reached that place, however, both the old man and the hut had completely vanished. And he could only find a few traces of a ruined hut there.

a poor father's legacies

Once upon a time there lived three brothers with their old father. Although they were well off in childhood, the family had gradually become poor. So when the father died, he could not leave anything valuable to his sons, except several objects as a token of his paternal love.

The three brothers agreed to divide them up equally. The strong, eldest brother took a pair of portable grinding stones, the middle brother took a walking stick and a dried hollow gourd, and the youngest brother took a *janggoo* [traditional drum].

Soon after their father's funeral, the three brothers decided to go out into the wider world. They wanted to make a success on their own. They agreed to get together again in their home village when they had made a big fortune.

In the early morning the three brothers set out, carrying their father's legacies with them. Before long, they reached a point where the path forked three ways. Each chose a different branch: the eldest took the left one, the middle brother the middle one, and the youngest the right one. Having reminded each other of their promise, they went on their way.

The eldest brother hurried off, and after several days

he found himself walking along a mountain path. When night started to fall, his legs were aching and he felt very exhausted. He could go no further. So he decided to spend the night on the mountain.

Looking around, he spotted a big old tree nearby. He thought he would sleep under the tree that night. A few moments later, however, he was suddenly gripped by the fear that he might be attacked by a wild animal or robbers during the night. So he changed his mind and he decided to sleep in the tree instead.

He began climbing up the tree, his bundle of grinding stones on his back, its strings tightly knotted cross his chest. When he reached a fork in a thick branch, he rested his grinding stones there and leaned against the tree trunk. Soon he started to doze off.

In the middle of the night, he was awakened by noises from under the tree. 'What on earth can those noises be, deep in the mountains?' he thought. He pricked his ears to hear more clearly.

'Is this all that I'm getting? Why's my share so small?'

'Because you didn't do much during the robbery.'

'I didn't do much, you say? You told me to keep watch while you robbed him.'

Below the tree two dark figures were arguing about dividing what they had robbed. Then the eldest brother, in the tree, had a very good idea. He started to turn one of the grinding stones against the other. This made a loud rumbling sound.

'What's that? What's that noise?' said one of the robbers.

'It's from up there. It's like thunder . . . Oh, it's the wrath of heaven!' replied the other.

'Nonsense! There hasn't been a cloud in the sky. So, how can—'

Before the robber could finish what he was saying, the eldest brother pissed on the thieves below him.

'You're right! Rain and thunder, out of blue! It must be the wrath of heaven.'

'Come on, run! Run for your life!'

The thieves ran away, scared out of their wits, leaving their booty. The eldest brother could hear faintly that they were still arguing as they ran away.

'It was your fault. You were so unfair about my share.'

'Oh, shut up! The wrath of heaven was against us both.'

When the thieves had gone, the eldest brother climbed down out of the tree. There he found gold and silver coins and jewels scattered on the ground around a wooden chest, which was almost full of such coins and jewels. He collected the coins and jewels, and put them back into the chest. Carrying the chest on his back, he returned to his home village.

The middle brother wandered about aimlessly for several days. One day, at dusk, he was passing by a graveyard. As he was tired and not sure about which way to go, he decided to spend the night there. He chose one of the biggest tomb mounds. He sat down and leaned his back against it, with the walking stick and the gourd by his side. Feeling snug and protected from the wind, he immediately fell asleep.

Deep in the night, the middle brother was awakened by the sound of footsteps. It was pitch-black, and the sound was coming nearer and nearer towards him.

He held his breath, frozen with fear. The footsteps stopped just in front of him.

'Just a moment! I can smell a live human somewhere,' said a voice.

'It can't be. We're in the middle of a graveyard, and it's a pitch-black night,' said another voice.

'Anyway, we should be cautious. We don't want people to know our plans, do we?' said the first voice.

'No. Never. Why don't you check it yourself, then?' said the other voice.

'Good idea! Let me feel the body. I can easily tell whether it's dead or not.'

At that moment the middle brother felt his heart sink. He was so afraid that he thought he would choke to death. But just then, a good idea struck him.

Immediately he held out the walking stick in the direction of the voices.

'Hm, the arm is very bony and dry . . . But I need to check further, to make sure.'

This time the middle brother held the dried hollow gourd, just in front of his head.

'Oh, it's a skeleton. I'm sure it's been dead for a long time. So we can discuss our plans here.'

From the two voices the middle brother learned that these figures were messengers from the underworld. And the next person to die was to be a sick young lady of a rich family in a nearby village. But they were hesitating to take her soul to the underworld.

'I feel sorry for her. Really! She's so young and so beautiful,' said the first voice.

'Me, too. But it's her fate, isn't it?' said the second voice.

The first voice said: 'Why don't we give her three more days? Her parents are doing everything they can to help her recover. I can't take their daughter away from them tonight.'

'Me, neither . . . It's really absurd, you know. Why didn't they think of using mugwort? It's growing everywhere. Having some bowls of mugwort decoction might revive her.'

'That's also part of her fate, isn't it?' said the first voice.

'Anyway, let's drop the subject and leave here now, before dawn breaks.'

As soon as the two underworld messengers had gone, the middle brother breathed deeply and relaxed. And as dawn started to break, he rushed to the rich family in the nearby village and told them the cure for the daughter's illness.

When she had recovered as the result of the mugwort decoction, her rich father arranged for her and the middle brother to be married. He gave them half his wealth and property. Now, as a rich man, the middle brother returned to his home village with his wife.

The youngest brother was heading for the capital city of the country because he thought he would have a better chance of success there. One day, as he was passing through a village at the foot of a mountain, he saw a public notice about a huge reward for catching a man-eating tiger. When he asked about the notice, an old villager said, with a sigh: 'Yes, a big tiger comes down the mountain every day and takes one person away with it. Soon this village will become a ghost village.'

Thinking of the tiger, the youngest brother hurried on his way through a forest. He started to feel exhausted, partly because of the drum slung at his waist. When he looked down at it, however, he had a surge of musical inspiration. So he started to beat the drum rhythmically.

Then, to his astonishment, a big tiger appeared out of the forest, several steps in front of him. The youngest brother immediately stopped where he was. But he continued to beat the drum, in order to overcome his extreme anxiety.

The tiger walked towards him in a strange manner, swaying to and fro. Its tail was gently wagging from right to left and left to right. The youngest brother realised that the tiger was dancing, instead of pouncing on him. So he went on playing the drum, more and more enthusiastically.

He walked towards the next village, where the people were amused to see the dancing tiger following him.

They collected coins and handed them to him. When the youngest brother and the tiger arrived at another village, the same thing happened. And so it went on from village to village. People watched them in amusement and collected money for the youngest brother.

At last the youngest brother reached the capital city with his tiger. And before he decided where to go, two men in uniform approached him.

'His majesty has summoned you and your tiger,' said one of them.

The men had been sent from the palace. So the youngest brother had no choice but to follow them.

When he was brought into the royal court, the king spoke to him in person: 'Word has spread that you have a very unusual tiger. A dancing tiger. Let me see it actually dance.'

So the youngest brother started to play his drum, even more fervently than before. The tamed tiger danced to the drum in a jolly way. The king was very amused and excited by this unusual performance. Furthermore, he wanted to keep the tiger in the palace. So he suggested to the youngest brother: 'Why don't you leave the tiger here? I'll give you as much money as you want for it.'

At first the youngest brother rejected the king's offer, saying modestly: 'I'm really sorry, your majesty! But the tiger is a family treasure. So . . .'

But the king was very keen on obtaining the dancing tiger, so he had a huge amount of money brought in and placed before the youngest brother. Thinking of the promise he and his two brothers had made, he accepted the king's offer.

The youngest brother returned to his home village with the money. There all the brothers met together again and lived in that village happily ever after.

the grateful magpies

A long time ago there lived a young man in a remote provincial village. Even though his parents were very poor, they did everything they could to help him prepare for a government administration exam. After many years of hard study the young man became confident that he could take the exam. So he departed on foot for the capital city of the country, to sit that year's exam. And he took with him a bow and arrows in case he encountered robbers or wild animals on the way.

Every day the young man hurried on his way as his destination was very distant and the journey would take many days. One day, in the late afternoon, while walking along a mountain path, he heard some magpies making a disturbing noise. They were darting up and down restlessly around a nearby tree. When he went nearer, he saw a serpent slithering towards a magpie nest. And from the inside of the nest he could hear the chirping sound of baby magpies.

The serpent had almost reached the nest and it would devour the baby birds at any moment! Immediately the young man pulled an arrow from his quiver and shot it at the serpent, which fell down onto the ground, dead.

Then the young man went on walking. But dusk was already spreading over the mountain. And before he had gone very far, it had become quite dark. He walked faster, trying to find somewhere to stay for the night, but he could not see any sign of houses or people.

'Oh, what shall I do in this wild place?'

When he had almost given up hope, he saw a light glowing in the distance. Feeling hope revive in his heart, he hurried in that direction. As he came near to the light, he realised it was coming from a hut.

'Ah, I'm safe now. They wouldn't be mean to a tired wayfarer. For just one night, they will surely allow me to stay there, even in their shed.'

When he reached the hut, a slim young woman welcomed him warmly. She even provided him with a big, delicious dinner. As soon as he finished the meal, he felt very sleepy.

The young woman offered him a small room, next to the main room. As soon as he went into the room, he fell into a deep sleep. But, in the middle of the night, he felt something tightening around his chest and neck. He could hardly breathe. He opened his eyes. To his surprise, a serpent was coiling around his body, with its head just above his own head.

'You killed my husband,' said the serpent in a hissing voice.

'Killed your husband? What do you mean?' he said, almost choking.

'Every evening, on his way back home, he rings the temple bell near here. Then I can get his dinner ready. But, today, I didn't hear the bell.' The serpent paused for a while, and added in a grave manner: 'You were the only one who came from that direction today. So, you must have caused some harm to him.'

Then he remembered the serpent he had killed on his way earlier that day. The young man said, feeling even more choked: 'I didn't mean to kill your husband. I just wanted to save the baby magpies.'

The serpent tightened its hold around the young man's body more tightly as it spoke: 'From tomorrow we are due to escape completely from our lives as serpents. But you have spoiled everything. You killed my husband!'

The serpent insisted on killing the young man unless they heard a sound of bell before midnight, which was almost upon them.

'Dong! Dong!'

All of sudden the bell rang, once and then twice.

'Oh, my husband's alive! Oh . . .'

The serpent uncoiled itself from the young man. And it slithered quickly out of the room.

As soon as dawn broke, he hurried to the temple bell. There, he discovered two magpies on the ground, just below the bell. They were both dead, with blood on their heads.

the golden axe
and the silver axe

Long ago a good-natured woodcutter lived with his elderly mother in a small village. Even though he was very diligent, he could not escape from his poverty. But he never failed to prepare a substantial meal for his mother.

One day he went into a thick forest to find some good firewood. He wanted to earn a sufficient amount of money so that he could buy food ingredients to cook a good supper for his mother.

After a while he discovered a suitable tree to chop down. It was a big tree standing by a pond.

The woodcutter started to strike the tree with his axe. Once, twice, three times . . . The tree was so big that it would not fall down easily. The woodcutter felt exhausted and he was sweating.

After resting for a while, he raised his axe again, over his right shoulder. However, just as he was striking it down towards the tree, it slipped out of his sweaty hands and fell into the pond.

'Oh dear!' he said to himself. 'What shall I do? That is the only axe I have.'

Fortunately, he saw a long stick lying on the ground nearby. With this he stirred the water in the pond, but he could not find his axe. He burst into tears, as he could not afford to buy a new axe.

By then, mist had started to rise from the pond, and in this a mountain spirit appeared. He looked very imposing, in a white robe, with a long pointed white beard, holding a rugged, dark wand upright in his left hand.

'Why are you crying?' asked the spirit.

'I dropped my axe into the pond. I've lost it.'

'You're crying just about that?' the spirit asked again.

'Now I can't get any firewood, so I can't buy food or anything.'

The woodcutter sobbed.

'Let me find it for you.'

Saying that, the mountain spirit vanished into the pond.

Very soon, he rose up again with a glowing golden axe in his right hand. As he raised it up, he asked: 'Did you drop this axe?'

The woodcutter shook his head and said: 'Mine is not golden.'

The mountain spirit disappeared again, in a flash. When he soon reappeared, he had a silver axe in his hand.

'Did you drop this axe?'

The woodcutter shook his head and said: 'Mine is not silver.'

And he told the mountain spirit that what he had dropped into the pond was not such a valuable axe, but an old iron axe. Touched by the woodcutter's honesty, the mountain spirit gave him the golden axe and the

silver axe, as well as the iron axe. So he returned home happily with these axes.

A greedy young man in his neighbourhood heard this story. He envied the woodcutter. So he hurried into the forest with an old iron axe. As soon as he arrived at the pond, he threw the axe into the water and pretended to cry.

The mountain spirit soon appeared and showed the man a golden axe. The man lied, telling the spirit that it belonged to him. When the spirit showed him a silver axe, the man lied again, saying that it too belonged to him. At that very moment the axes suddenly vanished from the mountain spirit's hands.

The spirit scolded the man and soaked him with water. The greedy man could not even get his iron axe back.

the spring of youth

Once there lived an old couple in a village near the mountains. The couple made a living by picking medicinal herbs and selling them in nearby markets. As they were kind, everybody in the village liked them.

The old couple had a happy life together, except for one thing: they had no children. They had always wanted very much to have children of their own.

One day the old man went to the mountains, as usual, to pick medicinal herbs. Luckily, he found a large patch of herbs near a big pine tree. And, while collecting them, he heard a bird singing. Looking up at the pine tree, he saw a bluebird at the top of it.

'Oh, bluebird! You sing very sweetly,' said the old man to the bird.

Suddenly the bluebird stopped singing.

'Oh, I'm sorry. Did I disturb you?'

As he said this, he unconsciously untied a scarf around his neck and wiped the sweat from his forehead with it. At that moment the bird darted down and picked the scarf from his hand.

'What on earth are you doing?' the old man shouted.

The bluebird flew back up, but didn't perch in the pine tree. It flew off to another tree a short distance away.

The old man ran towards the tree, shouting: 'Come back! Give me back my scarf!'

When he reached the tree, however, the bird flew off again to yet another tree. The scarf was still in its beak.

As the bluebird did the same thing again and again, the old man thought he should give up his scarf. But he could not . . . It was a special scarf, a gift from his old wife. Besides, he felt that the bird seemed to be leading him deliberately to some place. So he continued to follow the bird.

After going a long way, the bluebird dropped the scarf onto a large rock and flew away.

'Oh . . . at last . . .'

Completely exhausted, the old man sat down on the rock and picked up the scarf. And, at that very moment, he caught sight of a clear spring behind the rock.

'Ah, water! Spring water!'

Feeling parched, the old man scooped up some water with his hands and drank it. Strangely, he felt as though he had drunk some rice wine. He was confused and tired, and soon fell asleep.

When he woke up, it had already become dark. He started to walk hurriedly back home. Somehow he felt his steps were quite light.

Meanwhile, his wife was waiting anxiously for him at home. As he had not returned before it became dark, she went to their neighbour, an elderly widower, to ask a favour. She asked him to help her look for her husband, but he flatly refused to. The widower was a mean man and always envied the old couple's good relationship.

The wife decided to look for her husband herself. She went out in the direction of the mountains, carrying a small lamp.

When she reached the foot of the mountains, she saw a young man walking down towards her with a herb basket. And he was wearing the special scarf which she had given him around his neck. He looked exactly like her husband when he was much younger.

'Ah, darling, what are you doing here?' said the young man.

The old woman was very confused. She did not understand what was going on.

'What on earth happened to you?' she asked anxiously.

'What do you mean, what happened to me?'

'Your face! You look so young!' she explained briefly.

'Young?'

As he spoke, the man felt his face and looked at his hands.

'Now I understand what happened.'

He told his wife about the bluebird and the spring water. Then she realised that it was the Spring of Youth. And she also wanted to become young again, just as young as her husband.

Straightaway her husband took her to the spring. And he let her drink just as much water as he had done.

The next morning the widower in the house next door saw a young couple in their courtyard, instead of the usual elderly couple.

'That's strange! What happened to the old couple? Something terrible must have befallen them. Last night ... Oh, when the woman asked me to ...'

Regretting somewhat his unkindness to the old woman the previous evening, the elderly widower went to the couple's house. He wanted to know what had happened, and who the new young neighbours were. As soon as he heard about the magical spring, however, he set off directly to find it, taking with him a big ladle made from a dried gourd.

He did not come back again that day. The couple next door worried about him all night.

The following morning, the couple set out hurriedly for the Spring of Youth, in order to see what had happened to the widower. When they reached the spring, they found only a baby boy beside it.

The baby was lying in a man's jacket, and there was a pair of trousers beneath it.

'Oh, how cute! He's such a beautiful little baby,' said the wife. And she added: 'Anyway, where's our neighbour?'

'I can guess what happened,' said the husband. 'Look at the clothes. They're the man's clothes. I think he drank too much of the spring water.'

'Oh, so he became too young!' the wife responded with a laugh.

'Yeah, far too young!' The husband also laughed.

Then they were silent for a while, until the husband said: 'Why don't we take the baby home and bring him up ourselves?'

'Bring him up ourselves?' responded the wife.

'Yes, we always wanted so badly to have a child, didn't we?'

'We did, indeed.'

So the couple took the baby to their home and brought him up with much love and care. He grew up to be a kind, warm-hearted man.

rose and lotus

Long, long ago there lived a nobleman, named Moo Ryong Bae, in the north part of Korea. He was very well off and had a beautiful, good-natured wife. They had such a happy relationship that everybody in the town envied them.

One problem, however, was that they had no children. Even though they had been married several years, the wife had not conceived. The couple wanted a child so desperately that their life seemed empty without one.

One spring day, when the sun was shining and there was a balmy breeze in the air, Lady Bae felt drowsy. She started to doze off in her bedroom. Then she heard a voice, saying: 'My lady, allow me to present you with this flower!'

As she looked up, a heavenly maiden was standing there with a red rose in her hand. Behind her was hanging a beautiful rainbow. As the lady reached out her hand, the heavenly maiden handed the flower to her in a gentle manner. But suddenly a whirlwind swept the heavenly maiden away, together with the rainbow.

Surprised, Lady Bae woke up. It was a dream. The dream was so vivid that she could still smell the gorgeous scent of the rose. She wanted to share this unusual dream with her husband.

As soon as he heard about the dream, his face brightened and, holding her hands, he said: 'My dear, that seems to be a dream about conception. Oh, heaven has had pity on us and has blessed us with a baby!'

Indeed, before long the wife showed signs of pregnancy, and in due course she gave birth to a pretty baby girl. Remembering their dream, the parents named the baby Rose.

Two years later the wife had another dream, in which the heavenly maiden presented her with a lotus flower. She became pregnant again and gave birth to a second baby girl. In accordance with the dream, they named her Lotus.

Both Rose and Lotus were pretty, bright and gifted. And they had such a good relationship that they would even share a single soybean together. Whenever their parents looked at them, they were overcome with feelings of happiness.

The four of them led a happy life together until one day, some years later, a grievous misfortune struck them. The mother became very ill, and there were no medicines or treatment available to cure her. So eventually she died.

During the mourning period of three years, Rose and Lotus made an offering of food in front of their late mother's grave. They never missed a single day, whether it was sunny, rainy or stormy. And their sorrow at their loss became even deeper after the mourning period.

When the mourning period ended, their father's

relatives and friends recommended him to remarry. They even sent matchmakers to his house. Through one of them he was finally persuaded to marry a widow, even though he still missed his late wife and he was concerned about his daughters.

The new wife was younger than the first wife and quite well educated by decent parents. But she was not as attractive as the first one. She was a big, round woman with frog eyes, a big nose and thick lips. She had a loud voice and lost her temper easily. Also, she had three sons of her own.

Since their father remarried, Rose and Lotus had become quieter and more reserved. Most of the time they stayed alone in their own rooms, letting no one know what they were doing. Each time their stepmother approached them, they kept away from her.

She was disappointed and told her husband about it several times. Whether he was listening or not, he just kept silent. And, increasingly, he visited his daughters' rooms and spent more time with them, whereas he hardly spent any time with his new sons.

His new wife felt that she was being ignored and started to hate her stepdaughters. As time went by, her hatred grew uncontrollably. Eventually she decided to get rid of them. But how?

One day, a marvellous idea struck her like lightning. And the perfect opportunity came several days later.

That night her husband was not back home, and the daughters and sons had all gone to bed. The stepmother quietly called her eldest son, Jangsoe, out of his room to a corner of the courtyard. She whispered something into his ear. Jangsoe nodded several times, and went into the granary.

Before long he came back, holding a big, fat rat upside down by its tail between his thumb and forefinger. In the corner of the courtyard he skinned the rat and cut off its tail. His mother took the gory mass into Rose's room, and put it in her bed.

When her husband returned home late at night, she heaved a sigh with a hardened face.

'What's wrong?' he asked. 'Has anything happened to our family while I've been away?'

'You wouldn't believe it, so I'd better not talk about it.'

'What is it? I should know everything about what's happening in this family, shouldn't I?'

The stepmother opened her mouth, with pretended reluctance.

'It's our daughter, Rose . . . She has brought disgrace on our family.'

Her husband just glared at her.

'Recently Rose has been behaving strangely, so I have watched her for some time. Today she was very lazy and lay in her bed most of the time.'

The stepmother paused for a while. And, after clearing her throat, she continued: 'I wanted to know what her problem was. So I went to her room, and, Oh dear . . . how should I put this?'

'What? What happened? What's wrong with her?' her husband said anxiously.

'She . . . um, she had a miscarriage.'

'Miscarriage! What do you mean miscarriage? She's not married.'

'Exactly.' The stepmother sighed and continued: 'I couldn't believe it myself. But there's evidence of it in her bed.'

She got up determinedly and went out of the room. Her husband followed her. When they entered Rose's room, she was sleeping soundly. The stepmother walked towards the mattress and carefully lifted one corner of the sheet. Lying there was a gory mass!

'Oh, it's horrible, horrible, horrible!'

As soon as the couple returned to their room, the husband flopped down on the floor and just repeated the word 'horrible'.

'So what should we do about it?' asked his wife. 'Before the neighbours notice it, we should do something about the girl Rose.'

'What do you mean, do something about Rose?'

It was hard for him to believe that Rose had done such a horrible thing. She mainly stayed home alone or spent time with her younger sister Lotus. But . . . but, there was convincing evidence in her bed!

He was deep in thought, until his wife said: 'According to custom, she ought to commit suicide. But, I think, she's such a sly and shameless girl that she wouldn't do that. Instead, she would continue to live and bring more disgrace on our family.'

Then the stepmother made a suggestion to him. He reluctantly nodded in agreement.

They called Rose to their room and told her that she had to visit an uncle immediately, together with her stepbrother Jangsoe. She hesitated to obey them as it was in the middle of night and the uncle lived a long way away. But her father was very angry for some reason, so she could not refuse.

Two horses left the village, with Jangsoe and Rose on their backs. It was quite dark, but Jangsoe was carrying a torch which lit up the road ahead of them. Rose, though, could not tell what areas they were passing through. The route was unfamiliar to her.

After a while, they reached a thick forest on the side of a hill.

'Whoa, whoa!'

Jangsoe suddenly brought his horse to a halt, and signalled to Rose's horse to stop as well. The sound of an owl came from somewhere nearby. And Rose spotted a large pond below them in the dark.

'You should alight here,' Jangsoe said to Rose bluntly.

'What do you mean, alight here? This is not uncle's house,' Rose retorted. 'Where on earth are we now?'

Jangsoe looked at her sharply, without giving any answer. Rose felt her heart sink. Jangsoe looked so fierce that she could not help dismounting from her horse.

'Now, jump into the pond!' Jangsoe ordered.

'But, why?' Rose asked meekly.

'You have disgraced our family.'

Rose did not understand what Jangsoe was talking about. But she kept silent lest she provoke him.

'You have sinned by having a secret affair and, as an unmarried maiden, you miscarried a baby.'

Rose was dumbfounded. She tried to find words to protest. At once, however, Jangsoe went towards Rose, who was shaking and stepped back, falling into the pond.

Soon there was the thudding sound of water splashing from below. And . . .

At that very moment a chill wind arose in the forest, and a tiger sprang out of a bush. Alarmed, Jangsoe tried to escape onto the back of his horse, which immediately galloped away with the other horse. With one bound the tiger pounced on him, tearing one ear, one arm and one leg off his body. Then it sprang back into the bush.

At home, Jangsoe's mother was waiting anxiously for him to return. But, as his horse came back without him, she strongly suspected that something had gone wrong. She sent servants urgently to the pond area, where they discovered Jangsoe lying on the ground unconscious. They brought him back home.

When his mother saw him in such a terrible condition, without his right ear, his right arm and his right leg, she flew into a rage. She blamed Rose unfairly for the unfortunate incident. Furthermore, she still wanted to get rid of her sister, Lotus, too, as soon as possible.

Lotus did not know what had happened to her sister at all. When Rose did not turn up after several days, she started to think that something must have befallen her. But nobody would answer her anxious questions about Rose, not even her father. He just sighed and kept silent.

Lotus had an unusual dream one night. In that dream Rose was flying towards the northern sky on a majestic golden dragon. As Lotus called out to her, at the top of her voice, again and again, Rose gazed down at Lotus. She looked very sad and she was shedding tears.

'Oh, my little sister! Oh, your poor thing! Now we can't see each other again. We belong to different worlds, far far away from each other.'

Rose was flying further and further, on the dragon.

'Rose, my big sister! Take me with you, please. Please!'

'No, no, Lotus. No human can cross the boundary between us. Goodbye. Take care of yourself!'

'No, no, Rose. Take me . . .'

Before Lotus could finish what she was saying, the dragon suddenly looked back at Lotus and roared like thunder.

At that noise Lotus woke up.

Since that day Lotus passed each day sighing and weeping. She didn't eat much or sleep very long. Her cheeks had sunk and her face was clouded all the time.

Lotus felt strongly that Rose must have died. But how, and where?

Weeks later, an opportunity came for her to find the answers to her questions.

That day her father and her stepmother were absent from home for many hours. There were no signs of any other stepbrothers, except the oldest, Jangsoe. For some reason he was walking up and down restlessly in the courtyard. He looked pathetic, with one ear, one arm, one leg and a walking stick.

Lotus hurried out of her room and went to him. Jangsoe stepped back, looking at her cautiously.

'Oh, dear brother. You look so nervous. Don't worry, as I wouldn't do anything to harm you,' Lotus said in a coaxing voice. 'Just one thing, I want to know . . . what happened to Rose? Where is she?'

Jangsoe's face turned pale. He tried to turn around and walk away. Lotus held him by his left arm and continued to speak: 'That night you went with her. So you must know. I won't blame you for anything, really. You have already been punished enough, by the tiger.'

As Jangsoe wouldn't say a word, Lotus added: 'It wasn't your fault. You had to do what you were told by our parents, didn't you?'

An expression of relief came over Jangsoe's face.

'I won't tell anyone what I hear from you. So tell me what happened to Rose, please.'

Eventually Jangsoe told Lotus everything about the death of Rose, and his mother's plot against Lotus as well.

Since that day, Lotus felt even lonelier, and more and more fearful of her stepmother. She wanted to be together with Rose whatever it cost.

One moonlit night she left home and walked all the way to the pond, in which her sister Rose had drowned. Standing over the pond, she prayed briefly and jumped into it.

Several days later, the local magistrate died during the night. A new magistrate was dispatched to the district, but he died on the first night. And several more new magistrates died in similar circumstances.

Word spread that ghosts were appearing at night in the magistrate's house. Now, nobody wanted to be appointed to the position of magistrate, except a brave official named Dong Ho Jeong. He strongly believed that usually the spirits of dead people roamed about in this world when they had died with unresolved resentment. He wanted to know who had experienced such resentment in that district. So he volunteered to take up the vacant position.

On the first night he ordered all the rooms to be lit brightly. And he was sitting in his bedroom reading a book with candles lit. Time was passing slowly and everything was quiet. There was only the occasional rustling sound of the magistrate turning over a page of his book. Even that sound was becoming rarer and rarer until it finally stopped. He had fallen asleep.

Then, at midnight, a gust of cold wind came into the room and shook the flames of the candles. Feeling cold, the magistrate woke up from his dozing. At the door, to his horror, were standing two young women with faces as pale as paper and their hair hanging down loose. They both looked very sad.

Controlling his horror, the magistrate asked as loudly as possible: 'Who are you?'

One of them replied: 'My name is Lotus, and this is my sister Rose.'

'By your appearance I can tell you don't belong to this world any more. Why on earth are you roaming about here and disturbing people so much?' the magistrate said, plucking up courage.

'That wasn't our intention, sir. We just wanted to let the magistrates know about our undeserved deaths.' The voice was clear and warm, as though it were coming from a live person. And it continued: 'We are very glad, sir, that now we have found someone to listen to us.'

The ghost of Lotus told the magistrate how her stepmother's conspiracy had brought about her sister's death, which had led to her own death. Having heard the story, the magistrate promised that he would investigate the incidents and see that justice was done. Thanking him, the ghosts vanished immediately like smoke.

The next morning Magistrate Jeong summoned three members of the Bae family: the father, the stepmother and Jangsoe. When asked about the death of Rose, the stepmother insisted that she had had a miscarriage as an unmarried girl and committed suicide out of shame. And as evidence she presented the mass of dried gore and flesh. The magistrate ordered it to be cut open. Inside, they found undigested grains in their husks and rat faeces. After hours of investigation, the stepmother and Jangsoe confessed their guilt.

For causing Rose's death the stepmother and Jangsoe were sentenced to death. And the father was released with a severe warning to be concerned about his family.

Straightaway, on leaving the court, the father arranged

to search for his daughters' bodies in the pond. At the bottom of it they were lying side by side, with a peaceful expression on their faces. The bodies were removed and buried side by side on a hill facing south.

Several nights later, the father saw Rose and Lotus in a dream. They bowed deeply to him and, smiling, waved their right hands to him in farewell.

the fly and the sparrow

Once upon a time, when even tigers enjoyed smoking and magpies talked with people, there lived some hardworking people in a small village. One year, in the autumn, they had an extraordinarily good harvest from their paddies and fields, due to the good weather. They had had many fine days and a proper amount of rain.

To show their appreciation to the heavenly god, the villagers organised a ritual ceremony under a big zelkova tree at the entrance to the village. They had prepared various food offerings for the god. The Kim family had brought rice cakes, the Lee family fruits, and the Park family meat. Other families had also contributed different things, including fish, a pig's head and incense sticks.

Now the village people were standing in front of the offerings table. The oldest man, with silvery beard, bowed down very low and all the others followed him. But then a fly appeared from behind the zelkova and landed on a steamed yellow corbina fish. As everybody stood up again, they saw the fly!

In fury someone shouted, 'Go away!' The fly moved onto the pile of apples, and then onto the pig's head. The people shouted again reproachfully. But the fly continued moving from one dish to next, tasting each one.

'Catch it!' someone yelled.

People at the front tried to catch the fly with their hands, but they failed each time. More people joined them from the back. They all chased the fly and, in the commotion, someone was pushed against the offerings table accidently. Wine spilled from the offering glass, the incense sticks fell down, and jujubes rolled all around. The table was turning into a messy pile of food. Still, more and more people joined in trying to catch the fly.

'Stop! Now! All of you, stand back!'

All of them froze and looked in the direction of the voice. The oldest man stroked his beard with dignity and continued:

'We'll report this damn fly for its blasphemy to the heavenly god.'

The rest kept silent and listened attentively.

'Oh, heavenly god, please punish this fly severely. It has contaminated our offerings to thee.'

Suddenly, there was the rumbling sound of a divine voice from above: 'Bring the insolent little fly to me! It deserves a very severe punishment.'

In awe of the god's order, the fly flew off and hid itself on the back of the zelkova tree. A little boy noticed it and told all the others. The fly took off again, and flew as fast as possible to save its life. But people chased it, using all means to catch it. An old lady had brought a basket from her home, a young man had brought a broom and an old man a fly-swatter. Other people had also brought different tools, including a stick, a spatula and a catapult.

Eventually the fly was caught and brought before the heavenly god.

'What an insolent creature you are! You know very well how badly you behaved!' said the god.

The fly shrank in on itself with fear. The god continued to speak: 'How dare you touch the offerings to me? You must be punished for that.'

As the god scolded the fly, he picked up a stick to beat the fly's forelegs. But, when he raised it into the air, the fly rubbed its forelegs together in a gesture begging for mercy. At the same time it said in a sobbing voice: 'It's unfair, my lord.'

'Unfair? Why unfair?' the god asked dismissively.

Plucking up courage, the fly managed to say: 'There was another creature that touched the food for the offerings before me.'

Puzzled by what the fly said, the god asked: 'What creature was that?'

'A sparrow, my lord.'

'A sparrow?'

'Yes, my lord.'

The god's face turned red. And his voice became louder and harsher.

'How dare you deceive me? No sparrow came anywhere near the table. So how could it touch the food?'

The god was so angry that the fly rubbed its forelegs together more vehemently. And immediately it said: 'I'm not lying, my lord. Please let me explain.'

Intrigued by the fly's suggestion, the heavenly god said bluntly: 'Go on.'

Hurriedly the fly explained that the rice cakes had been made with grains from the fields, but the sparrow had already tasted the grains before they were harvested. So the offerings had already been contaminated by the sparrow, even before they were placed on the table. Persuaded by the logic of the fly's argument, the god ordered the sparrow to be brought to him.

After a while, the sparrow was brought before the heavenly god.

'Why am I here, my lord?' the sparrow asked in a frivolous manner.

'You really don't know why?'

'No, my lord.'

'Really, you cheeky thing! I'll tell you.'

The lord cleared his throat, before continuing: 'You touched the rice grains in the field before they were harvested, didn't you?'

'I did. I was hungry, so——'

'How dare you! Each year the harvest should be offered to me first. But you touched some of it, so now you must be punished for this!'

The god raised the stick in the air. The sparrow attempted to walk backwards with quick, short steps. But the stick hit its left leg hard, and then its right one, and then its left one again . . . So painful was the beating that the sparrow started to hop up and down. Even after the bird was released by the god, the pain continued.

Back in the village, the sparrow happened to meet the fly by chance. Feeling sorry for the sparrow and in order to beg its forgiveness, the fly rubbed its forelegs together. On the other hand, the sparrow was reminded of the heavenly god's punishment and the pain in its legs. Unconsciously the bird started to hop up and down. So that's why sparrows hop around so much, and flies often rub their forelegs together.

the good brother and the bad brother

Once there lived two brothers, named Heungboo and Nolboo, in a prosperous farming family. Heungboo, the younger one, was gentle and generous in nature, whereas his elder brother Nolboo was greedy and mean.

From childhood Heungboo could not bear seeing people suffer. So he always shared his food with hungry neighbours, gave his coat to shivering beggars and carried things for old people.

By contrast, Nolboo did many mischievous things. Whenever he saw a beggar, he broke his bowl. He liked throwing stones at neighbours' soy jars, blocking sluice gates to rice paddies and knocking toddlers over.

When the brothers grew up and both were married, they still stayed in their late parents' house together. Over the years their personalities did not change much. Heungboo was still concerned about others, while Nolboo made every effort to increase the family's fortune. Day in, day out he worked hard supervising the ploughing, planting, watering and harvesting.

Each year the family's wealth accumulated like a rolling snowball. And Heungboo became more and more generous to people in need. This annoyed Nolboo unbearably.

On a cold winter's day Nolboo called Heungboo to his room. Even before Heungboo had sat down, Nolboo said, in an angry, harsh voice: 'I want you to leave this house today, with your wife and children!'

This came as a bolt from the blue for Heungboo. He knew his brother's personality well, but how could he do such a cruel thing to his own brother? Heungboo just begged Nolboo for mercy, saying in a subdued voice: 'It's the middle of winter now. So, brother, please allow us to stay here until spring comes.'

'Spring is far, far away. Can you imagine how much more of my food your family will waste before then?'

Heungboo reminded Nolboo of one important fact: 'Our parents repeatedly told you to look after your younger brother well, didn't they?'

This made Nolboo even angrier.

'Yes, they did. They asked me to look after you well. So I did, more than enough! Now you must stand on your own two feet. From today, from this very hour!'

'But how can I start a new life, without any preparation and in this cold season? Brother, please . . .'

'That's your problem, isn't it?'

Nolboo paused for a while, before continuing: 'While I was working in the fields, you spent your time reading. While I was saving every penny, you were wasting enormous amounts of money on beggars. You've already spent more than your share of the inheritance.'

Heungboo protested cautiously in a subbed voice: 'I don't think I've spent that much. In fact I wasn't generous enough to poor people.'

Suddenly, Nolboo struck the floor of the room with

his fist. Thump! Thump! Thump! Startled, Heungboo looked up at him with raised eyebrows.

'I don't want to listen to you any more. So leave, now, with your wife and children.'

As soon as he said this, Nolboo stormed out of the room.

From that cold winter's day, Heungboo's family wandered around trying to find a suitable place to settle down. People took pity on them, and gave them food and some clothes. Finally Heungboo found an old, derelict house in a village near his home village. The owner of the house allowed his family to live there free of charge.

The house was small and shabby. There were many holes in the walls, which caused chilly draughts. The roof was damaged so much that melted snow water dropped down into the rooms. So they were cold and damp.

For the first time in his life, Heungboo had to do odd jobs. As he didn't earn much, his wife also worked for the neighbours by doing washing and sewing. Although both worked hard, the family were barely able to live from hand to mouth. They were always hungry, and the children often complained, cried and fought for food.

Despite the poverty, however, Heungboo and his wife loved each other very much. And somehow they managed to have twins every year. So their money situation never improved, although they worked harder and harder every year.

One year, in the spring, the couple had another set of twins. Now they had twelve children altogether. With a mixture of happiness and worry, Heungboo was sitting quietly in his courtyard. Then, a couple of swifts arrived and hovered above the courtyard.

'Oh, dear,' murmured Heungboo. 'You'd better go to another dwelling. You won't find a suitable spot to build a nest on this shabby house.'

The swifts soon flew away.

The next day, however, the swifts came back. Each of them was carrying a piece of mud in its beak. And they started to make a nest in one corner of the roof, under the eaves. Flying busily to and fro, they brought mud, pieces of hay and feathers, and within a few days the nest was completed.

In the nest they laid six eggs, all of which hatched successfully. The baby swifts grew well during the summer period. When cool breezes started to blow from the west, they began to practise flying.

One morning Heungboo discovered that a baby swift had fallen down into the courtyard. All the other baby swifts had flown away to a southern country together with their parents. He examined it and noticed that one of its legs was broken. He hurried into the house and brought out a piece of cloth and some thread. Heungboo wrapped the broken leg in the cloth and tied it up with thread. Then he put the bird back into the nest.

For several days Heungboo fed the bird. And early one morning, he realised that the nest was empty.

The following year, on a fine spring day, Heungboo went into the courtyard and saw a swift on the roof. It had a cloth on its leg.

'Oh, you've survived and come back again. I'm really glad.'

The swift turned to him. It had something small in its beak. It flew up in the air and started to hover around above the courtyard. Once, twice, three times . . . It dropped the small object from its beak. Then it flew away.

Heungboo went to look at the object and realised that it was a gourd seed.

'Strange! Why did the bird drop this seed into my courtyard?'

Heungboo thought it was very unusual. There must be some reason for it! He decided to plant the seed near the right side of the house.

Several days later there was a shoot springing from the seed. It grew very fast. It thrived so well that it soon became like a thick bush. Heungboo set up some poles leaning against the roof. The tendrils and leaves of the gourd plant quickly covered the whole roof.

Soon three white flowers opened on the plant. They turned into gourds as small as a sparrow's head. But they grew quickly and became the size of a chamber pot, and then a large full moon.

By then it was almost time for the autumn festival of *Chuseok*. All the neighbours were busy making half-moon rice cakes, collecting jujubes and nuts, preparing meat dishes and buying new clothes. But Heungboo's family could not afford to do these things.

The children begged for new clothes, rice cakes and

sweets every day. Yet Heungboo and his wife could not do anything about it except comfort them. They felt so helpless . . .

Then Heungboo suddenly had a good idea.

When he told his wife about it, she agreed. So Heungboo climbed a ladder up to the roof and picked one of the three gourds.

His idea was to cut the gourds into halves, scrape out the flesh and cook it as a meal for the family. And they could sell the empty halves as bowls for keeping cereals or scooping water from a well.

So Heungboo and his wife squatted down in the courtyard, with the large gourd between them. Facing each other, they each held one end of a saw and started to cut the gourd in half.

'Here we're sawing a gourd
Pushing the saw hard
Pulling it again backwards.'

While the couple were sawing the hard shell, Heungboo started singing a rhythmic melody. Then his wife responded:

'Some have a wealthy life
We have a poor life
Now we need some food.'

While sawing the gourd, Heungboo noticed that his wife was not doing it hard enough.

'My dear, can you do it harder?' he said.

'Oh, I'm so hungry. I can't even hold the saw properly.'
His wife let go of the saw. Heungboo said: 'Let's try again. We're almost there.'

Heungboo encouraged his wife to tighten the sash

around her waist and try harder. She followed his advice and resumed the sawing.

Before long, they saw a bright gleam inside the gourd. And then it split into halves. Heungboo and his wife immediately closed their eyes, because of the brilliant light in front of them. When they opened them again, to their surprise, each half of the gourd was full of gold and other jewels.

Heungboo, his wife and their children danced around joyfully in the courtyard, hand in hand, arm in arm, or hugging each other closely. And when their excitement had died down a little, the couple continued to saw the second and third gourds in half.

The second gourd contained silk clothes and house appliances. And from the third one there came a group of servants and carpenters. They swiftly constructed a new home for the family, consisting of several imposing buildings.

Heungboo became one of the wealthiest men throughout the country.

The news spread quickly and reached Nolboo's ears as well. He was jealous of his younger brother rather than being happy for him. He wanted to get hold of his brother's fortune for himself.

But how?

He pondered on it for a while. Then, suddenly, a good idea occurred to him.

Immediately Nolboo rushed off to Heungboo's home. When he arrived, he was overwhelmed by the size and imposing appearance of the buildings. Very soon

Heungboo opened the gate himself instead of a servant.

'Hello, brother! How have you been? It's been a long time . . .'

Before Heungboo could finish his greeting, Nolboo cut in: 'Is this really your home? It's very difficult to believe.'

Heungboo just smiled and led Nolboo into the courtyard. Along the promenade there was a large pond with lotus plants, and in the middle of the pond an artificial island with a pavilion on it.

Heungboo took Nolboo into his drawing room. As soon as the two brothers sat down facing each other, Nolboo adopted an accusing manner and said: 'I heard that you and your family have been stealing from the neighbours regularly'

Heungboo was surprised at what Nolboo said, and protested: 'What? What are you talking about, brother?'

'If not, how could you make such a fortune? Tell me the truth. Then I'll help you escape to somewhere safe. An investigation is going on to find the thief.'

Heungboo wanted to tell him the truth, but Nolboo stopped him from speaking by holding out his right hand. And quickly he continued: 'I'll look after your house and your property. Everything. So, hide somewhere with your family for a while. When things have settled down, I'll call you back here.'

'No, brother.' Heungboo shouted. 'Never! I'm not a thief.'

And he explained to Nolboo about the swift.

'A swift? A gourd seed? Really? You're lying to me, aren't you?'

After Heungboo swore several times that he was not

lying, Nolboo left the house. As soon as he got home, he urged his servants to make artificial swift nests, as many as possible. They put dozens of the nests around the eaves of all the buildings.

The problem, however, was that it was autumn. All the swifts had already flown off to a warm country and they would not come back until the following spring.

Each day Nolboo anxiously waited for night to fall. And he counted how many days there were to go until spring.

Time went by so slowly. To Nolboo each day was like a whole year.

But, at last, autumn finished and winter came.

Somehow winter also passed, and finally a new spring arrived.

Early one morning Nolboo went out to the courtyard, and as usual waited for swifts. After a little while, he saw a couple of them flying in the direction of his house. To his delight, the birds flew straight into one of the nests on the main building.

Soon they laid six eggs, all of which hatched successfully. The baby swifts thrived during the summertime, and started to practise flight. They all flew around the house very fast. None of them failed in their flight practice and fell down into the courtyard. Now it was time for them to fly away to a warm southern country. It made Nolboo more and more anxious with each passing day.

One morning, before dawn, Nolboo placed a ladder under the nest of the swifts. He climbed up and put his hand into the nest. He caught one of the baby swifts and threw it onto the ground.

'Oh, dear, the poor thing! It fell out of the nest!'

He climbed down. The baby swift was lying on the ground with its chest and belly upward. Its legs were shaking in the air, and it cried in pain.

'Don't worry! I'll look after you.'

Nolboo pulled out a piece of cloth and some thread from his jacket pocket. He put the cloth on one of the swift's legs and tied it with the thread. Then he put the baby swift back into the nest.

The next morning, all the swifts, including the baby swift, had gone.

'Oh! Finally all of you went south. Come back next year and bring many gourd seeds.'

Each and every day Nolboo counted how many days remained until the next spring.

Eventually . . .

Spring finally arrived. And the swift, with the cloth patch and thread still on its leg, dropped a gourd seed into Nolboo's courtyard and flew away.

Immediately Nolboo planted the seed. The next day a shoot appeared, and it grew very quickly. Soon the plant bore a dozen gourds, each of which became bigger than the size of a full moon.

Nolboo was already preparing to cut open the gourds. Instead of having his servants do it, he squatted down in the courtyard with his wife, facing him, and with the biggest gourd between them.

He chanted impatiently:

'Here we go
Open now,
Open!'

The gourd was cut into halves very easily. To the great shock of Nolboo and his wife, some young men in armour jumped out of it and beat the couple mercilessly.

'It seems that we chose the wrong gourd. Let's try the smallest one this time.'

So a servant brought the smallest gourd to them. It was also opened without difficulty. And out of it came a big troupe of itinerant dancers and acrobats. While they were rehearsing their performance, they trampled all over the grasses and flowers in the courtyard.

And out of the third gourd there jumped a group of *dokkaebis*, wielding their spiky clubs. They completely destroyed the buildings and household equipment, and took away all the valuables.

Nolboo had become penniless.

Heungboo heard the news and invited Nolboo and his family into his house. Nolboo regretted everything he had done. And the two families lived happily together ever after.

how the hare escaped from the tiger

Long ago there lived a clever hare in a remote mountain. One autumn day it was taking a nap under a bush, when a tiger approached, trying to eat it. The hare opened its eyes and realised that the tiger was right in front of it with its mouth wide open. The hare was terrified. However, it thought quickly and said: 'Oh, hello! Where are you going? I've been waiting for you.'

Puzzled by the hare's words, the tiger just looked at it. Then the hare added hastily: 'Actually, I have some delicious rice cakes to give you. They're a very rare kind. Do you want to try them?'

Intrigued by the hare's offer, the tiger nodded.

Immediately, the hare collected several exquisite-looking pebbles. As it put them in front of the tiger, it said: 'I bet you never had such delicious rice cakes as these.'

'How do you eat them?' the tiger asked promptly, smacking its lips.

'It's quite simple. You just bake them on a fire. That's all you need to do.'

Then the hare made a fire and put the pebbles on it.

'You have to wait for a while, until they are well baked,' said the hare.

The fire blazed and the rice cakes seemed to be baking quickly. But the tiger was becoming impatient. The thought of eating the rice cakes made its mouth water. It swallowed saliva secretly, but the hare noticed it.

Smiling at the tiger, the hare said: 'They're nearly done. But . . . Oh dear, I forgot the honey. It will make the rice cakes even more delicious.'

The hare looked at the tiger cautiously. There was no change in its facial expression. So the hare continued: 'I'll be back in a jiffy, with some honey. Don't touch any of them. Do you promise me?'

'I promise,' the tiger answered quickly.

'There are six altogether. I've counted them,' the hare said, and ran off.

The hare did not return as soon as the tiger expected. He looked at the rice cakes. They seemed to be well baked. And to his joy, there were seven of them, not just six.

'The stupid hare! It miscounted them. So I can have one now, and it won't notice.'

The tiger hurriedly picked up one of the rice cakes.
'Ughhh!'
The pebble was so hot. Unbearably hot.
With burning pain on its tongue, the tiger jumped around madly for hours and hours.

Several days later, the hare encountered the tiger again in the middle of a field. Actually, the field was overgrown with eulalia, so the hare could see the tiger only when it was standing right in front of it.
'Oh, hello! How——'
'Cut it out!' the tiger roared. 'You tricked me last time. I'm still suffering from being burned by your "rice cake". You should be punished for that.'
The tiger opened its mouth to eat the hare.
'Wait a second, please,' the hare said as loudly as it could, stepping back.
'What now?'
'Actually, last time, it wasn't wholly my fault. You're also partially responsible for it.'
'What do you mean by that?'
As the hare managed to keep the tiger talking, it gave it some encouragement. It plucked up courage and said: 'The last time I asked you to wait until I came back with some honey. But you didn't, did you?'
'No, I didn't,' the tiger answered in a low voice.
'You see! So, you can't just blame me.'
The tiger felt that the conversation was going in a strange direction which it had not expected. But it could not figure out exactly what was happening.
The hare went on: 'Actually, there's something I want

to tell you. I was chasing sparrows. Did you know that they are an exquisite delicacy?'

'No, I didn't,' the tiger answered dejectedly.

'You should try them.'

The tiger smacked its lips, unconsciously.

'But the problem is . . .' the hare paused deliberately for emphasis before continuing: 'The problem is that these sparrows are very difficult to catch. I think I can't do it on my own. Can you help me? If we work together, we can get dozens of them, even hundreds. Just look around you.'

Indeed, there were many flocks of sparrows fluttering around in the field of dried eulalia plants. Looking at the hare, the tiger nodded in silence.

'Good! You just need to stand here with your mouth wide open. Then I'll chase the birds in the direction of your mouth. You can eat them even without touching them.'

The tiger readily agreed to the hare's suggestion. It opened its mouth wide. And the hare went off to chase sparrows.

Soon the tiger heard the hare shouting: 'The birds are coming. Lots and lots of them. Keep your mouth open. Turn your face to the sky and close your eyes. The birds are flying just above you.'

So the tiger did what the hare told it to do. It could hear a flock of sparrows fluttering and twittering. The sound came nearer and nearer. The size of the flock also seemed to become bigger and bigger.

Strangely, the tiger started to feel hot. It opened its eyes, only to realise that it was surrounded by a fiercely burning fire of dried culalia plants. It could not escape and its fur was severely burned.

So the tiger had to stay in its cave until the fur grew back again. All the time it felt furious about what the hare had done.

One winter's day the tiger was strolling far down the stream. The whole world was covered with snow, and it was very difficult to find prey.

Fortunately, a small animal was hopping along the stream towards the tiger. Hastily it ran to the animal and realised that it was the hare, which had tricked the tiger twice.

'Oh, you slimy little wretch! You humiliated me twice. But this time you will never escape from me,' said the tiger.

'I'm sorry. I really am. Now you can do anything to me you want. I deserve it,' said the hare in a subdued voice.

'Good! Then I'll eat you up.'

The tiger was about to pounce on the hare. But it had already stepped back a little and said: 'I really apologise and I want to compensate for my tricks.'

'Compensate? How?' asked the tiger.

'There are many fish in this stream. I'll help you catch them. Then, you won't have to worry about food all winter.'

The tiger frowned.

'Yuck! You eat fish?'

The hare replied: 'Yes. I live on them during winter. They're most delicious at this time of year.'

The hare paused for a second, before continuing: 'It's very difficult to find food in this season, isn't it?'

The tiger nodded.

'Well, you can catch fish at any time, and as many as you want.'

What the hare said was very tempting. But the tiger was determined not to be tricked by the hare again. So it said to the hare in an angry voice: 'You're going to trick me again so that you can escape from me, aren't you?'

'No, dear me! How could I? We've met three times within several months. I'm sure we will easily meet again any time in near future. At that time, will you forgive me for all these tricks?'

'No, never! This is your last chance.'

'You see? I wouldn't risk my life, would I?' said the hare.

This made the tiger confused again. He just managed to say bluntly, 'No.'

Then the hare said promptly: 'So, are you ready to catch fish?'

'You should tell me how,' responded the tiger.

'Of course,' said the hare. 'It's quite simple. Just put your tail into the water of the stream. It'll be like a bait to attract fish. When you feel the tail becoming quite heavy, pull it out. And you'll pull a lot of fish out with it.'

'But where will you be? You're not going to run away while I'm fishing, are you?'

'No, no, no! I'll sit by your side all the time.'

So the tiger did what the hare told it to do. The water

felt cold. And as the sun moved westwards, it felt colder and colder.

Gradually the tiger started to get bored and wondered how many fish had bitten its tail. It moved its tail a little. The tail felt quite heavy.

At that moment, the hare noticed it and told the tiger to be patient a little longer.

The sun had just gone down over the western hill.

'Now you can pull your tail out. There must be lots of fish on it,' said the hare, smiling all over its face.

The tiger tried to lift its tail out of the stream. But it was too heavy to be pulled out.

'Damn, too many fish!' it shouted, looking at the hare.

The hare moved away to a safe distance, and, still smiling, it said: 'Hee, hee, hee! It's not fish that have been caught, you stupid creature, it's you! The stream has frozen all over and your tail is stuck in the ice.'

The hare said goodbye and hopped away.

And the next morning a team of three hunters discovered the tiger, tied it up and took it away.

the forgetful *dokkaebi*

Once upon a time there was a seven-year-old orphan boy living in a little town. As nobody looked after the boy, he had to earn some money to support himself. He ran errands for the neighbours and got some tips from them.

One day the boy did errands for the organisers of a funeral. He was paid five *nyang* at the end of the day when he left for home. He hurried on his way, clutching the coins firmly in his hand.

When he turned the corner into his alley, he heard his name being called. He stood still.

Very soon someone called his name again, and clapped their hands twice.

'It must be a *dokkaebi*,' thought the boy. He had heard that *dokkaebis* usually call someone's name twice and clap their hands twice.

'But how can I escape?' the boy wondered.

Having realised that he had to face the *dokkaebi*, the boy turned around. There, standing in front of him, was just another boy . . . No! It was a young *dokkaebi*, without horns, and not much hair on its arms.

Smiling faintly, the *dokkaebi* said: 'Can you lend me just five *nyang*? I'm broke.'

Five *nyang* was all that the boy had with him. How could he possibly lend it to someone? But he was worried that the *dokkaebi* would do some harm to him if he rejected its request. So he handed the coins over to the *dokkaebi*, saying: 'You really will pay it back to me, won't you?'

'Sure. At this time tomorrow. So don't worry!'

And, with these words, the *dokkaebi* vanished like smoke.

That evening the boy could not eat a single morsel of food. He went to bed early on an empty stomach.

The next day the boy did just a few errands for the neighbours. He went back home a little earlier than usual and took a rest. Suddenly he heard someone call his name twice and clap their hands twice.

When he opened the door of his room, he heard the voice of the *dokkaebi* again, coming from behind the fence.

'Here's the five *nyang* I borrowed yesterday!'

There was a clinking sound. Five coins had been thrown over the fence into the courtyard.

The next day the same thing happened, again the day after that, and the day following that too. This continued for several months, so the boy became much better off.

One evening the boy was returning home, when he heard his name and the hand-clapping as usual. But the voice sounded dejected and the clapping was faint. When he turned around, the young *dokkaebi* was standing there with its head bent down.

'I'm sorry I still haven't paid you back the money I borrowed.'

The boy was confused, and very anxious. What if the *dokkaebi* had realised he had paid more than a hundred times as much as he had borrowed? So he just said: 'Actually you did. Remember?'

'No,' said the *dokkaebi*. 'I don't know why, but somehow my money bag became empty.'

The boy did not say anything. And the *dokkaebi* continued: 'Is it OK if I pay you back by giving you a cooking pot? I have plenty of new cooking pots.'

'Of course,' the boy answered immediately. He had only one pot, which was very old and rusty in many places.

'Thank you. You're a good friend,' said the *dokkaebi*.

Then it suddenly disappeared.

And from the next day a new cooking pot was thrown into the boy's courtyard every evening. His kitchen became full of pots, and now he had to pile them in his bedroom as well. He had to stop it urgently.

The boy thought about how he could stop the *dokkaebi* from bringing a pot every evening. Eventually he had a good idea. And, before long, he had the chance to put his plan into action.

One evening, the boy happened to meet the *dokkaebi* again. Before the *dokkaebi* could bring up the subject of the money, the boy said in a clear voice: 'Thank you for paying the money back.'

'Did I pay you?'

'Yes, you did. You definitely did.'

The *dokkaebi* just stood there, without speaking and looking confused. Cautiously, but trying to be casual, the boy continued hastily: 'You *dokkaebis* are strong and have magic powers. So, I guess you aren't scared by anything, are you?'

'Actually, we are,' said the *dokkaebi*. 'In my case, I'm scared by the head of a dead foal.'

After pausing a few seconds, the *dokkaebi* asked: 'So, what scares you most?'

'A *saekdong jeogori*. You know that short jacket with colourful stripes?'

The *dokkaebi* nodded. And the boy almost smiled, but managed to control it.

The next day the boy did not do any errands, but stayed home all day. At home he spent hours and hours drawing a dead foal's head. And, before sunset, he fixed the drawing on the fence around the courtyard. Then he waited quietly in his room.

After a while, he could hear the sound of the *dokkaebi* coming towards the house. Then the *dokkaebi* cried: 'Ughhh! A dead foal's head . . .'

The boy heard the *dokkaebi* running away hastily.

The following evening there was a thud in the courtyard. The angry *dokkaebi* had thrown a pile of *saekdong jeogori* over the fence. And they were the very clothes the boy had always dreamed of wearing.

the good girl and her stepsister

Long ago there lived a man called Mr Choi in a southern province of Korea. He had been happily married for twenty years, but had no children. Both he and his wife wanted a child so much that they prayed to the moon for days, weeks and months . . . Eventually the couple had a daughter, and named her Kongjui.

Kongjui was very beautiful. And she smiled as beautifully as a heavenly maiden. When her parents looked at her, all their troubles melted away like snow in the spring sunshine. Every moment of every day they spent happily.

Unfortunately, however, their happiness did not last long. Kongjui's mother fell ill unexpectedly and died soon afterwards. It was on the one-hundredth day after Kongjui's birthday.

Kongjui's father made every effort to bring up Kongjui well. Their neighbours also felt compassion for her, so young breast-feeding mothers suckled Kongjui in turn.

Kongjui grew to be a beautiful, sensible girl. She was also so gifted that she started to manage various household jobs at around age ten. Her father was very proud of her and doted on her.

When Kongjui turned fourteen, her father started to think seriously about her future. He could not keep her with him for ever. She would marry one day and leave him. That thought made him feel lonely and insecure. Kongjui sensed this and encouraged him to remarry, by saying emphatically: 'Don't worry about me, Father.'

Kongjui's father was really encouraged by her words and eventually remarried. His new wife was a widow with a daughter of her own. She was plain-looking and only seemingly good at housekeeping. And her daughter, named Patjui and one year younger than Kongjui, was a plump girl with a dark skin and pockmarks on her face.

Both the mother and the daughter were nasty and cunning. When Mr Choi was around them, they pretended to treat Kongjui generously and fairly. However, as soon as he stepped out of the gate of their house they bullied her around and forced her to do all the household work. And now the stepmother started to bully Kongjui to do farm work as well.

One spring morning Mr Choi was getting ready to leave home on business. While his new wife was helping him, she called Kongjui and Patjui to the main bedroom.

'Hey girls,' she said in a mellow voice. 'Your father is away from home today on business. So I want the two of you to weed our fields, just for a few hours. They are overgrown with weeds . . . All right?'

'Yes, Mother,' Kongjui and Patjui responded simultaneously.

As soon as Mr Choi had left the house, beaming contentedly, his new wife handed a hoe to each of the girls: a new iron hoe to Patjui, and an old wooden hoe to Kongjui. And she allotted a sandy field to Patjui and a gravelly field to Kongjui.

Patjui finished picking weeds from the sandy field before lunchtime. But Kongjui just managed to finish only one furrow of the gravelly field by then. She was not confident of finishing all the furrows by sunset. She worked harder and harder, and more and more hurriedly.

Then, unexpectedly, her wooden hoe broke.

'Oh, dear!' Kongjui sighed. 'What am I to do? I'll most certainly be punished for this. And my stepmother won't give me any dinner.'

Kongjui began to sob in the middle of the field. At that moment there was a sudden flash of light in the sky and an ox with sable fur was standing in front of her.

'Why are you crying?' asked the ox with a deep 'Moo'.

Startled by the sudden, mysterious appearance of a speaking ox, Kongjui wanted to run away. But, strangely, she could not move a single step. Then, somehow her fear disappeared and she felt at ease with the ox. So she said: 'I have to weed this field before it gets dark. But my hoe's broken.'

'Don't worry about that. Just go to the brook over there and wash the tears off your face. Then we'll see,' said the ox.

Kongjui did what the ox asked her to do. When she went back to the field, to her great surprise, it had been completely weeded. And a new iron hoe was lying where the broken wooden hoe had been.

The ox had vanished into thin air.

Several weeks passed.

It was in the early morning of *Dano*, the May festival. Kongjui's stepmother and Patjui were wearing new dresses and busily putting on make-up. Kongjui changed quickly into a fresh, clean dress and waited for them to be ready.

'Fancy going on a swing today, do you?' asked the stepmother warmly.

'Yes, Mother,' replied Kongjui. She really wanted to go on a swing with other girls in the festival. She also fancied watching healthy young men competing in *ssireum* [wrestling] and a tug-of-war.

'I tell you what,' said the stepmother, still speaking warmly. 'First, draw water from the communal well and fill the water jar in the kitchen. Then you can join us in the festival.'

It seemed to be a very generous offer. In order to fill the jar, which was half the height of Kongjui, she only needed to make a few trips to the nearby well.

No sooner had the stepmother and Patjui left the house than Kongjui dashed to the well with an earthenware pot. She drew water in a bucket, poured it into the pot and hurried back to the house. Then she poured the water into the jar in a dim corner of the kitchen.

One pot, two pots, three, four . . . seven . . . ten!

There was no sign of the water rising to the brim.

'What's wrong?'

Anxiously Kongjui looked into the water jar and spotted a small, lighter-coloured part in the bottom. It was a hole and through it the water was draining out.

'Oh, what am I going to do?' muttered Kongjui, sobbing. 'My stepmother will go mad if I go to the festival with the jar left empty.'

Kongjui began to stamp around anxiously. At that very moment a toad crept out of another dim corner of the kitchen.

'Don't worry, Kongjui. I can help you,' said the toad. 'If I block the hole under the jar, you can easily fill it.'

'But I don't want you to get hurt. You might even be killed.'

Even though Kongjui refused to accept the toad's suggestion, it insisted strongly: 'I've lived for hundreds of years. That's more than enough.'

Kongjui still hesitated. Then the toad went on: 'Don't worry about me. I'm going to die soon, anyway!'

Reluctantly, Kongjui agreed with the toad. And, while she tilted the water jar, the toad crept under it.

The jar was filled in a few minutes. And Kongjui ran to the festival site. When her stepmother heard from her that the jar had been filled, she would not believe it. And she said to Kongjui reproachfully: 'Surely some men must have helped you secretly. And you gave them your favours as a reward.'

Several days later Kongjui's family were invited to her uncle's party. Kongjui was walking on air in expectation of seeing her mother's brother. It had been such a long time since she had seen him last.

In the morning, before the party, Kongjui's stepmother went into her room and said: 'You also want to go to the party, don't you?'

Kongjui nodded, with a pleading look.

'Then you can follow us later. After you finish weaving the hemp cloth and husking three sacks of rice.'

The stepmother went out of the room and took Patjui to the party. Kongjui's father had already set off to the event. And now Kongjui was left at home alone with a large amount of work.

Kongjui spread three sacks of unhusked rice onto the straw mats in the courtyard. She had to wait for the grains to dry completely in order to husk them. In the meantime, she went to her room to begin weaving the hemp cloth. She would have to make several more feet of it.

'Oh, how can I finish this before it gets dark?' she sighed. 'And I also have to deal with the rice later.'

She looked out of the door and saw a large flock of sparrows pecking at the grains in the courtyard.

'I'm so unhappy. I won't be able to go to the party. Oh, why are those birds bothering me like that?'

Exasperated, Kongjui burst uncontrollably into tears. At that moment a beautiful woman in a silk robe appeared, out of nowhere, in front of her.

'Kongjui!' said the woman in an echoing voice. 'I know you want to go to the party very badly.'

'How do you know that?' asked Kongjui.

Instead of answering the question, the beautiful woman said: 'You must hurry if you don't want to arrive there too late. Here!'

She produced a bundle wrapped in a silk cloth. When Kongjui opened it, she found a set of new clothes, a hair ribbon and a pair of silken shoes with a flower pattern.

'I don't deserve these things . . .' Kongjui paused for a

few seconds and continued: 'I have work to finish.'

'Don't worry. Leave it to me.'

The beautiful woman went towards the loom. Her hands and feet moved very elegantly and quickly. Soon she had woven a long piece of cloth.

'There! It's done! I hope you have a good time at the party.'

With that, the woman vanished in a cloud of rainbow-coloured smoke.

'Thank you, beautiful lady. But I still have to husk the rice now.' Murmuring this to herself, Kongjui stepped down into the courtyard. To her surprise and joy, all the rice grains had been husked. The sparrows were not eating them but pecking off the husks.

'Oh, thank you, sparrows! Now I really can go to the party.'

Kongjui hurried out of the house in her new clothes, hair ribbon and silken shoes. They fitted her perfectly. As she walked, she felt as light as if she were flying.

In the fields and over the hills, many colourful flowers had blossomed. Butterflies were fluttering around and bees were busy collecting honey. Kongjui was attracted by pretty flowers and beautiful butterflies, but she had to hurry to reach her uncle's house. She ran along the stream.

When Kongjui turned at a bend of the stream, she suddenly heard a resonant voice somewhere behind her: 'Hey, there! Clear the way!' Looking around quickly, Kongjui realised that it was the new magistrate arriving in procession.

Immediately she turned to the left and tried to find a place to hide herself, as she was in awe of the magnificent procession. But she could not find any bush or shrub nearby. So she began to cross the stream to reach the other side. By accident the silken shoe on her left foot fell off. Before she realised this, the shoe was floating away, out of reach.

In the meantime, the procession came near the bend. The magistrate looked out of the palanquin and happened to spot something pinkish floating in the stream.

'Halt!' he ordered from his palanquin. 'Go and fetch that pink object over there.'

He pointed towards the shoe. And one of his young footmen dashed down to the stream, grabbed the shoe and brought it back to the magistrate.

'Oh, it's beautiful!' exclaimed the magistrate. 'Who can have lost such a gorgeous shoe? Someone who likes wearing this kind of shoe must have very good taste.'

He issued an order to his attendants: 'When we arrive at my new official residence, do everything you can to find the owner of this shoe. She must be very sad to have lost such a precious item.'

As soon as the procession reached the residence, a group of attendants set off to find the owner of the shoe. They visited many different villages, but failed to find the owner. At dusk they reached the house of Kongjui's uncle.

Noticing that there was a party going on, one of the attendants said hopefully: 'The shoe owner must be here. It's a style of shoe only worn on special occasions.'

They entered the courtyard, and the head attendant clapped his hands to get attention. Everybody at the party turned to look at him. Then he explained why they were there.

Suddenly there came a loud voice from one of the tables: 'The owner's here!'

The attendants and guests turned towards the table. A plain-looking woman was pushing forward a plump girl with dark skin and a pockmarked face. The girl's mouth was still full of food. It was Patjui.

Swallowing the food quickly, Patjui said in a very exultant voice: 'Yes, that's mine.'

'Then why don't you prove it? Put your foot in the shoe so that we can judge it.'

The silk shoe was lying on the step to the main building. Patjui tried to put her left foot into the shoe, but the shoe was too small. She pushed harder and harder.

'Hey, you'll tear the shoe. Obviously you're not the owner,' said the head attendant.

'Yes, I am. Definitely!' protested Patjui. 'I lost it some time ago. Today my feet are bigger because I walked a long way to come to the party.'

'How dare you lie? Do you know what punishment you will get if you interfere with the magistrate's work?' said the head attendant angrily.

Patjui stepped back. Then an old lady waved to the head attendant, who went towards her. She said to him: 'Didn't you notice a charming girl at this party who's wearing only one shoe?'

'No, madam.'

'She was here just now. But where's she gone?'

The old lady looked around, and she said exultantly: 'There she is.' she pointed to Kongjui, who was hiding behind a group of people near the step. She was wondering why the magistrate wanted to find the owner of shoe.

To her relief, the head attendant spoke to her in a very polite and warm manner: 'Would you please come forward and put your foot in the shoe?'

When Kongjui did as he asked, everybody could see that it fitted her foot perfectly.

'At last, we've found the rightful owner of the shoe,' exclaimed one of the attendants.

And they asked Kongjui to come with them to the official residence.

When the magistrate saw Kongjui, he lost his heart to her completely. He could not control himself, and proposed to her on the spot: 'Will you marry me?'

Kongjui was also attracted to the handsome young magistrate. So she nodded shyly.

Several weeks later, a grand ceremony was held. And Kongjui and the magistrate lived happily together until, one day, Patjui suddenly visited them.

At that time Kongjui was taking a walk around the pond in the back garden. The moment Patjui saw Kongjui, she rushed to her and said: 'How have you been, sister? I've missed you every day since you got married. I couldn't wait any longer to see you. So here I am.'

Kongjui was touched by Patjui's words. Now she wanted to forget all the bad things that had happened in the past.

'Sister!' Patjui continued in a warm voice. 'I deeply regretted how badly I treated you! I really felt rotten about it.'

Patjui pretended to wipe tears from her eyes. Kongjui took hold of Patjui's hands firmly to comfort her. Patjui held Kongjui's hands even more firmly and pulled her to the pond.

Splash!

Both Kongjui and Patjui had fallen into the water. Kongjui tried to get out, but Patjui kept pushing her deeper and deeper into it. Kongjui's feet were now sinking into the muddy bottom of the pond. She struggled desperately to paw the water with her hands, ducking up and down, up and down . . . Then her head disappeared completely under the water.

In the evening, as the magistrate returned from his office, his 'wife' greeted him in a quiet voice. She was standing to one side, and she looked somehow strange.

'Are you all right? You seem a little different this evening,' said the magistrate.

'Yes,' replied his 'wife', still speaking quietly. 'I was outside in the back garden all afternoon. The sun was too strong for my skin.'

'I see,' said the magistrate, relieved. 'Then be careful from now on.'

Several days later, the magistrate noticed that his chopsticks on the dinner table did not match each other. He called a maidservant and complained: 'These are not a pair. How can I eat with them?'

At that very moment, the echoing voice of a young lady was heard from outside: 'You noticed that the chopsticks don't match each other. But why don't you notice that you and your wife are also not a pair?'

It was Kongjui's voice, and it was coming from the direction of the back garden.

Immediately the magistrate rushed out of the room and into the garden. But no one was there. He looked around anxiously. He could not see a single soul. But, in the pond, he saw a large lotus flower, strangely larger than the other flowers. And it had an unusually bright pink colour.

'What's that?' he murmured to himself. 'Why does that flower stand out so distinctively from the others?'

He ordered the flower to be picked and brought to him.

Two servants approached the lotus flower in a boat. They were surprised to find, under the flower, a human body in the water with its face upward. They pulled it out of the water.

It was Kongjui's body. And it seemed to be far too late to bring her back to life. There was no other choice for the magistrate but to bury her.

In a solemn atmosphere, Kongjui's body was cleaned, and now it was being dressed in a shroud. In order to put the sleeves on the arms, the head and the upper back had to be raised from the table. Then, to the undertakers' astonishment, Kongjui's bosom heaved and sank down . . . again . . . and again . . .

Suddenly Kongjui opened her eyes. She had come back to life!

Having heard what had happened to Kongjui, the magistrate vowed to take care of her more attentively.

He showed deeper affection for her, and Kongjui also treated him more kindly and more warmly.

Over the coming years they had four children, and they all lived happily together.

a bride for one grain of millet

A long, long time ago there lived a young bachelor in the central region of Korea. Actually, he was not very young, but well into his thirties. He was very clever and smart, but very poor – so poor that no girls in his village and its vicinity wanted to marry him.

One day he decided to leave his home to find a wife elsewhere. He made several pairs of straw shoes for the journey, but he had no food to take with him, except one grain of millet. It had been left in the cereal jar in the granary. So he set off on his journey.

On the first day, as the sun was setting, he went to a tavern to find a room for the night. As he was going to bed, he asked the tavern owner to keep the grain of millet safe until he asked for it the next morning.

'Don't worry. You'll get it back intact,' the tavern owner promised. However, thinking the request was really absurd, the owner threw the grain of millet away into the courtyard.

The next morning the man asked for the grain of millet back as soon as he got up. The owner searched every inch of the courtyard, but could not find it. So he offered to give the man one of his millet grains instead. But the man flatly rejected the offer, saying: 'My millet grain was an unusual one. It was special and very valuable.'

The owner thought up an excuse: 'But a rat has eaten it up. So what can I do about it?'

'Bring the rat, then!' said the young man firmly.

So the tavern owner had to catch a rat. And the young man left the tavern, taking the rat with him.

He went through many villages, crossed many streams and climbed over many hills. As it got dark, he went to another tavern in a quiet town. Having finished his simple dinner, he asked the owner's wife to keep the rat safe during the night. And he went to sleep.

Thinking this was rather weird, the woman put the rat in the storeroom. During the night a cat sneaked into the storeroom and ate the rat.

In the morning the man asked for his rat, and the woman told him the truth. And she offered to catch another rat for him. But he insisted on having the very same rat he had asked her to look after for him.

'Oh, dear, dear! Your rat is already in my cat's stomach. So how can I get it for you?'

'Then let me take your cat with the rat inside it.'

The woman had no choice but to give the man the cat. The man took the cat and left the tavern immediately.

At the next tavern he stayed, the owner's foal kicked the cat to death. So the young man demanded that he be given the foal. And, with the foal, he continued on his way through many more towns, fields and woods. In the next tavern, the owner's ox butted the foal in the stomach, giving it a fatal wound. So the man obtained the ox and set off on his journey again. He still had not found a suitable wife yet.

At dusk he reached a big market town. There he discovered an inn with an old shed, where his ox could stay that night.

The next morning, he got up a little later than usual. He still felt tired, probably because the day before he had walked a long way with his ox. And, to his surprise, the ox had disappeared. Soon he found out that the innkeeper's son had sold it in the marketplace. He had to pay back his gambling debt of the previous night.

'I'm really sorry,' the innkeeper apologised. 'You can take my ox instead.'

'No. I must get my own ox back. For me, it's a special ox.'

So the innkeeper rushed to the marketplace, only to find out that the ox had already been butchered. It was to provide meat at a banquet for the birthday of a local nobleman's daughter.

'Then I should take the person who ate the meat,' the

young man insisted. 'Please lead me to the nobleman's house.'

The man was so persistent that the innkeeper had no choice but to take him to the nobleman's house. When the nobleman heard the young man's demand, he thought it was ridiculous. However, he noticed signs of cleverness in the young man's eyes. And he was impressed by his sheer courage and incredible persistence. So he allowed the young man to marry his beautiful daughter. That was how the poor but clever bachelor got a wife.

the serpent bridegroom

Once upon a time there was a woman who had no children. She wanted a child so badly that she even thought she would not mind a serpent as a baby. And eventually she really did give birth to a serpent.

She could not keep the serpent baby in the house because she worried about the neighbours seeing it. So she put it below the chimney in the backyard and covered it with a bamboo hat.

The three daughters of a neighbour heard that the woman had had a baby. They wanted to see it. But when they saw it, the two eldest girls felt disgusted and spat at it. However, the youngest one consoled the crying serpent baby and kindly covered it with the bamboo hat again. Despite the contempt of other people, the serpent baby grew up well. Then, one day, he wanted to get married.

When his mother heard of this, she said firmly: 'Look at you! Who in the world would want to marry you?'

But he pestered his mother to ask the neighbour's daughters to consider it. After several days' hesitation, she told the girls' mother about his wish.

The girls' mother thought it was a joke and told her daughters. The eldest daughter laughed and flatly rejected the proposal, saying: 'I'd rather stay a spinster for ever.' And the second one also rejected the serpent's proposal, saying: 'I would rather die than marry him.' But, to everybody's surprise, the youngest one accepted his proposal. So she soon married the serpent.

During the wedding night the serpent asked his bride to heat water in a cauldron. With the heated water he took a bath. When he stepped out of the bath, he had been transformed into a handsome young man with fair skin and an imposing physique.

In the morning everybody was lost in admiration for his wonderful transformation. And the bride's two sisters became very jealous of her. Everybody could see they were very happy together.

Several years later, the husband had to go away for a while to take the examination to become a government official. As he set out, he handed a small bundle wrapped in white paper to his wife.

'What's this, dear?' asked the wife.

'This is my cast-off skin. Please look after it well. Don't lose it or let it be burned. Otherwise, I won't be able to come back.'

As soon as he said farewell to her, she hid the small bundle in her bosom lest it be seen by others.

A couple of days later her sisters visited her. They noticed there was something bulging at her bosom and forced her to show it to them. She refused stubbornly. Then the eldest sister twisted her arm behind her back, while the other one pulled the bundle from her bosom.

She hurriedly opened the bundle and exclaimed: 'Yuck! It's disgusting!' And the eldest one added: 'Why do you keep it on your body? You're sick!' Then the second sister immediately threw the serpent skin into the courtyard and set fire to it. It burned up in no time, and the smoke, with a distinct smell, writhed away.

Now it was well past the time when the husband should come back, but he had not. A day, a week, a month went by, and another month, and yet another month . . . But the husband still did not come back.

Finally, the wife decided to go around and try to find her husband for herself. But she had no idea where he might be. So she had to walk endlessly, making enquiries, wherever the path took her.

One day, late in the afternoon, she reached a stream and saw a large flock of crows swarming around on a sandbar. Raising her voice, she said to them: 'I'm looking for my husband. He's wearing white trousers and a jade-green overcoat, and he's very good-looking. Have you seen anyone like that around here?'

'If you wash these maggots clean for us, we'll let you know. They must be as clean as jade.'

So the wife washed a pile of dirty maggots clean. Then one of the crows pointed to a hill slightly further upstream, saying: 'You'll find a wild boar over there. He'll let you know.'

After the wife had walked along the stream for a while, she caught sight of a wild boar at the foot of the hill.

It was laboriously pulling something out of the ground.

'Hello!' said the wife. 'I'm looking for my husband.' And she explained to the wild boar what her husband looked like. Then the wild boar responded, saying: 'If you dig up this thick arrowroot and clean it thoroughly for me, I'll tell you.'

So the wife had to spend quite a while digging up the thick arrowroot and washing it thoroughly. Only then did the wild boar point further upstream, saying: 'You'll find an old woman over there. Ask her.'

Further upstream she found a shabby old lady washing her dirty clothes. When the wife asked her about the whereabouts of her husband, the old woman asked her to wash all the clothes. So the wife used all her energy to wash the dirty, heavily stained clothes. Then the old woman gave her a rice-bowl lid and one chopstick, and said: 'Get on this rice-bowl lid and row with this chopstick. Go against the flow of the stream, as far as its source. Beyond that point is his house.'

Suddenly the rice-bowl lid did not look small, and the chopstick began to look like a sturdy oar. After the wife had been rowing the lid for a while, she found herself surrounded by flowers with subtle fragrance. The lid rolled from side to side, and the bride became unconscious.

Then . . .

A spectacular scene unfolded in front of her. In the distance were hills with green trees and colourful flowers, and near her there were wide fields with abundant crops and grazing cattle. Beyond the fields there was a big tile-roofed house, lit up by the sunset.

The wife hurried to the house in excitement, only to

find that the gate was firmly locked. She called out loudly. After a minute, a young maidservant opened the gate.

The wife begged desperately: 'Can I spend the night in the house, please?'

The servant replied: 'You can come in. But I can't put you in a room. You'll have to sleep under the wooden floor of the servants' quarters. There's only space for you to crawl in, next to the family dog.'

The wife appreciated the offer and followed the maid into the courtyard. The maid pointed to a hole under the floor of a building. Then she brought a bowl of food remains. The wife gobbled it up and instantly fell asleep in that space, as she had had a long, hard day.

Soon, however, she woke up to the sound of a voice: 'Missing her so badly.'

The voice was coming from the drawing room. And she could see the silhouette of an imposing young man on the paper screen of the door.

After a short pause the voice started to recite poetic phrases again:

'Oh moon, so bright
And the stars too.
I feel so lonely
Missing her so badly.'

Immediately, in reply, the wife also recited poetic phrases:

'Oh moon, so bright
And the stars too.

*I am so tired
Looking for my husband.'*

No sooner had she finished her recitation than the door of the drawing room opened and a man dashed out.

'Oh, my wife's around here somewhere! Is it a dream, or is it reality?' he said exultantly.

'It's reality, my dear!' said the wife, crawling out from under the servants' quarters. And husband and wife embraced each other.

The wife explained to the husband what had happened to his cast-off serpent skin. And he explained that he had not gone back to her because he thought she had burned it herself out of disgust. So all their misunderstanding were resolved, and they lived together happily ever after.

from corn cakes to riches

A long, long time ago there was a rich nobleman who had a poor servant. The nobleman was so concerned about money that he even went to bed with a money bag under his head. And he only allowed his servant to have one small, cheap corn cake for each meal. So the servant was always hungry.

The nobleman saved money in every way he could. And the servant collected all the crumbs left from his corn cakes, keeping them in a sack. Whenever the nobleman saw his servant doing it, he laughed at him and said disdainfully: 'You stupid man! What's the use of all those crumbs?'

Yet the servant continued to collect the corn-cake crumbs, and eventually the sack became full of them.

One year, in the summer, it rained constantly for one month and one week. Paddies and fields were flooded, and roads and houses were swept away. All the village people escaped to the top of a nearby mountain. The nobleman took his money bag with him, and the servant took his sack of corn-cake crumbs. The nobleman made fun of the servant, saying: 'You stupid man! What's the use of bringing that sack?'

The rain continued to pour down heavily. With no

food available, the people on the mountain felt so hungry that they would have chewed leather.

On the fifth day the servant opened his sack and ate some of the corn-cake crumbs. The villagers asked for some crumbs too and he could not refuse. But the nobleman did not want to humiliate himself by begging for some crumbs.

The servant occasionally opened his sack and ate some crumbs himself. Each time, the nobleman watched him doing it, and finally he could not help asking for a handful of them. The servant rejected his request, saying: 'I thought this kind of cheap food was only for humble servants, like me, not for noble people like you, master!'

The nobleman offered him several coins, but the servant would not accept them. Then the nobleman

doubled his offer, but the servant still would not accept the money. So he offered more and more money for the crumbs, but each time the servant flatly rejected it. The nobleman felt that he would starve to death. So finally he offered the servant his whole bag of money for a handful of the corn-cake crumbs. Now the servant accepted his offer.

Soon afterwards the rain stopped. The nobleman realised how ridiculous he had been. After that, he was never mean again. Instead he became generous and friendly.

the cat in a palanquin

Once upon a time there lived a farmer, Mr Jin, in the north part of the Korean Peninsula. He was just managing to survive with his wife and daughter, Yeon-hee, but he was very sympathetic to anyone in distress.

One day, on his way back home from his fields, he discovered a gaunt kitten at the roadside. It looked very weak, with much of its fur fallen out.

'Oh, you poor thing!'

Mr Jin could not just pass by the poor kitten, so he lifted it up in his arms.

When he brought the kitten home, his wife got angry, pointing out that they did not have enough food to share with a kitten. But Yeon-hee wanted the kitten very much. So she pointed out that when the kitten grew up, it would catch the rats which stole their rice. Her mother eventually allowed her to keep the kitten.

At each meal Yeon-hee shared some of her food with the kitten and took good care of it. Over several weeks it grew healthy, and after some months it became fully mature. But the cat never wanted to catch any rats. It usually just dozed and did not bother, even though rats passed by right in front of its eyes. So rats boldly frequented Yeon-hee's house.

Very disappointed, Yeon-hee's mother drove the cat out of the house by brandishing a poker. But, each time, the cat sneaked back into the house.

When Yeon-hee grew up, her parents arranged an engagement between her and a hard-working young man in a neighbouring village. And as the wedding day was around the corner, the parents wanted to provide her with a good costume and throw a generous party by selling the rice in their granary. When they opened it up, however, they realised that all the rice had gone.

'What's happened to our rice?' exclaimed Mr Jin.

'Oh, what should we do now?' cried his wife.

As their eyes gradually became accustomed to the dim light in the granary, they noticed there were fat rats swarming in one of the corners. They had eaten all the rice.

Out of despair, Mr Jin fell ill.

Yeon-hee nursed him day and night. She tried to console him by saying: 'The wedding can be postponed, Father. Until then we can work hard and save a lot of rice again, can't we?'

In spite of Yeon-hee's devoted nursing, however, her father became worse and worse.

In this situation, Yeon-hee's lazy cat did something very unusual. Late one morning it loitered around in the courtyard, and suddenly dashed into the main room. It brought out a piece of hemp cloth and entered the granary with it. Putting it on its head, like a mourner's hood, the cat started to wail loudly.

Wondering what the wailing was about, the rats started to gather around the cat. And one of them asked: 'What on earth is the matter?'

'My father died last night . . . Oh, Father, Oh, Oh!'

'Did you have a father? I didn't know that,' said another rat.

'Don't be silly! Everybody has a father, don't they?' said the cat. And, pretending to be sad, it began to wail again.

'Oh, I'm sorry. My condolences!'

'My condolences!'

'My condolences!'

The rats showed their sympathy for the cat as they remembered that it had never tried to kill them.

'By the way,' said the cat in a clear voice. 'Where are your manners? How come you express your condolences empty-handed?'

'Oh, we're sorry. We'll be back soon with our contribution to the funeral,' said the first rat. And he said to all the other rats: 'Let's leave now.'

Soon each of the rats brought some rice to the cat.

Having heard about the cat's father, all the rats in the village also brought some rice. And the rats in the neighbouring villages brought some, too. Finally the King Rat came to show its respects to the cat's father.

The cat could tell it was the King Rat because of its big, sharp teeth and longer whiskers. No sooner had the rat said, 'My condolences!' than the cat pounced on it and pressed it hard with its right front paw.

'Oh, Oh, what's the matter with you? You treated us well, but why this sudden change of attitude?' the rat protested. The cat said emphatically: 'You don't know how fierce I can be. By midnight, you must take all the rats in this area into the mountains. Never return to the village. If you do, I'll kill every single one of you. Understood?'

'Yes,' replied the King Rat. 'Spare my life, please. I'll take all the rats right away.'

As soon as the rat was released from the cat's paw, it scurried out of the granary, through a hole in a corner. And the other rats dashed helter-skelter after it.

The next morning the cat tugged at Yeon-hee's skirt hem with its mouth and led her into the granary. To her surprise and joy, it was full of rice.

'Oh, am I dreaming?'

Impulsively, Yeon-hee held her cat in her arms and danced around in the courtyard.

Hearing the good news, Yeon-hee's father started to recover quickly from his illness. After several days, he was completely cured.

And . . .

Yeon-hee's wedding proceeded according to the original plan. Her palanquin, decorated with flowers, took her out of her house and through the alley. The procession moved from her village towards the bridegroom's. Behind her palanquin there was another palanquin, small and cute.

'What's that extra small palanquin for?' asked someone in the crowd.

Someone else lifted up the awning of the palanquin and said: 'It's her cat!'

Inside the small palanquin Yeon-hee's cat was dozing contentedly.

the mud snail lady

A long, long time ago, when tigers also enjoyed smoking, there lived a young widower in a farming village. He was lonely and often fell into a melancholy mood.

One day the young widower was weeding his rice paddy. And in the middle of his work he sighed and said to himself: 'What's the use of all this hard work? Who will eat the rice with me?'

Suddenly, out of nowhere, came a faint voice: 'I will. Who else?'

The man turned round, but he could not see anyone. 'That's strange,' he thought. And he said again, in a slightly louder voice: 'Who will eat the rice with me?'

'I will. Who else?' It was the same voice again, from the bank of the paddy field.

When the man went towards the voice, he could find nobody there except a big mud snail. It was just pulling its feeler back into its shell. The man picked it up and brought it back to his home. He put the snail into an earthenware jar in a corner of the kitchen. Then he poured water into the jar.

The next morning the young widower went out to work in the farm as usual. When he started to feel hungry, he returned home to discover that a bowl of freshly cooked rice and side dishes had been set on the table. He was so hungry that he started to eat the food without thinking about who had prepared it.

He had never had such a delicious meal!

The following day the same thing happened again, and the day after that as well. He wondered who on earth was doing this.

One day he returned home earlier and hid himself in a corner outside the kitchen to find out who the person was. He kept peeping in. Near lunchtime, to his surprise, a beautiful lady emerged out of the earthenware jar. She made lunch swiftly, and set the table.

When she was about to go back into the jar, the man rushed into the kitchen and confronted her.

'Who are you?' he asked.

The lady did not reply.

'Why are you hiding in my kitchen . . . in that jar? And why are you cooking for me?'

'I mustn't talk about it. It's not the right time yet. Please give me some more time.'

The lady looked at the man with pleading eyes. He nodded.

'One important thing!' the lady said. 'You shouldn't peep at me. So please leave me now.'

The man went out of the kitchen immediately. There was something dignified and graceful about the lady which prevented him from challenging her.

The man strove to keep his promise by concentrating on his farm work. But it was too difficult. All day long the image of the beautiful lady haunted him.

One morning he pretended to go to work and hid himself in the corner outside the kitchen. He peeped inside frequently. Before too long, the lady's upper body emerged from the jar, naked. She was washing herself.

She was so beautiful that the man could not control himself. He dashed into the kitchen and held her hands with his.

'Whoever you are, will you marry me?' he said with heartfelt emotion.

Pulling her hands back, the lady said: 'I wanted you to wait three more days. But you've broken your promise.' She paused, and then, sighing, continued: 'I'm one of the daughters of the Dragon King under the sea. I was exiled to the land for making a serious mistake. I'm being punished, and in three days my punishment would have ended. But . . .' The lady paused again before clearing her throat and resuming her speech in a sobbing voice: 'You spoiled everything. Now I can't become a real human. Why couldn't you be a little more patient?'

Her eyes were brimming with tears. And her body suddenly started to shrink, becoming smaller and smaller.

'Oh, Oh, what's happening?' the young widower exclaimed.

Very soon the beautiful lady had shrunk down into the jar. When the man looked inside it, he could only see a simple mud snail on the bottom.

why the sea is salty

Once upon a time there lived a king who had a pair of magical grinding stones. They provided whatever the king required them to. He wanted to boast about them to his government officials. So one fine spring day he held a special banquet, during which he had the grinding stones brought in.

When the officials were seated, their glasses were filled with fine rice wine. And as soon as they made a toast, the king had the officials pay attention to him.

'I'm going to show you all an extraordinary thing,' said the king. And he turned to the grinding stones and said: 'I order you to produce gold.'

The upper stone began to turn by itself, and immediately gold nuggets poured out from between the upper stone and the lower stone. Then the king held out his hand above the stones, and they stopped. The officials were so amazed that they could not put their feelings into words.

With a contented smile the king turned again to the grinding stones and said: 'I order you to produce pearls.'

Immediately hundreds of pearls poured out, gleaming exquisitely.

'Oh, it's amazing, your majesty!' one of the officials exclaimed. Then other officials competed with each other to express their admiration as strongly as possible. Carried away by a feeling of triumph, the king continued to produce many other precious things with his magical grinding stones.

And as the banquet was about to end, he demanded a

pledge from all the officials. So they solemnly promised not to tell anyone about what they had seen at the banquet.

Somehow, however, the secret leaked out. And word about the king's grinding stones spread from person to person, village to village, and eventually throughout the kingdom. A thief on a remote island also came to hear about it.

Several days later the thief climbed over a wall of the palace in the middle of the night. He sneaked into the king's bedroom and stole the magical grinding stones. In order to escape from the commotion among the royal guards, he hid himself in a storeroom. And he fled the palace the following night.

He hurried off with the grinding stones on his back. Eventually he came to a seashore and spotted an empty boat. He put the grinding stones in the boat and started to row it into the sea. When he had reached a point where nobody could see him, he thought about what he wanted to obtain from the grinding stones first.

Salt!

Salt was so rare that he could become a wealthy man if he had a large amount of it. So he hastily chanted: 'Give me salt!'

The upper stone immediately turned by itself and began to produce salt.

'Oh, it's really salt!' he exclaimed. 'Yes, salt! I want more of it.'

The stone started to turn faster and faster, and produced a larger amount of salt.

'I want more, more, more . . .' the man shouted exultantly.

Soon the boat became full of salt, and it started to roll from side to side. But the thief continually shouted for more salt without noticing this. Finally, the boat could not bear the weight any longer and began to sink.

Only then did he realise that he had to stop the grinding stones, but he did not know how to.

So he drowned. But the grinding stones have continued to turn endlessly at the bottom of the sea ever since. And that is the reason why the sea is so salty.

also published by hesperus minor

Hesperus Minor is committed to selecting well-loved children's books from the past and introducing them to a whole new generation. All of our books are published in beautiful editions for the whole family to treasure.

The Children of the New Forest	Frederick Marryat
The Coral Island	R M Ballantyne
The Life and Adventures of Santa Claus	L Frank Baum
The Lost Prince	Frances Hodgson Burnett
The Nutcracker	E T A Hoffman
Pollyanna	Eleanor H. Porter
Pollyanna Grows Up	Eleanor H Porter
The Prince and the Goblin	George MacDonald
The Prince and the Pauper	Mark Twain
Puck of Pook's Hill	Rudyard Kipling
Rebecca of Sunnybrook Farm	Kate Douglas Wiggin
The Runaways	Elizabeth Goudge
The Story of the Treasure Seekers	E Nesbitt
Tanglewood Tales	Nathanial Hawthorne
The Wouldbegoods	E Nesbitt
The Blue Fairy Book	Edited by Andrew Lang
The Green Fairy Book	Edited by Andrew Lang
The Red Fairy Book	Edited by Andrew Lang
The Yellow Fairy Book	Edited by Andrew Lang

www.hesperuspress.com/hesperus-minor.html

the story of the treasure seekers
by e. nesbit

£7.99 • ISBN 9781843914747
foreword by julia donaldson

From the author of *The Railway Children*, an enchanting adventure in the company of the inventive and mischievous Bastable children – Dora, Oswald, Dicky, Alice, Noel and H.O. – who plot to restore their father's fortune by any means possible.

This is the story of the different ways we looked for treasure, and I think when you have read it you will see that we were not lazy about the looking.

'Even though they wear the stiff formal clothes of the late Victorians, eat cold mutton and sago pudding, write on slates and read forgotten books, their feelings are timeless and are so powerfully described that any modern child could identify with them.'
— Julia Donaldson, author of *The Gruffalo*

the lost prince
by frances hodgson burnett

£7.99 • ISBN 9781843914815
foreword by matt haig

Whenever Marco Loristan walks down the road, people turn to take a second look. He is unusually tall and handsome for a twelve-year-old boy. Brought up to respect his elders, with a keen artistic eye, a talent for language and a solid moral compass, he is shaping up very well. But change may be on its way as the situation in his homeland of Samavia starts to alter. Will he be allowed to serve his country as he dreams of doing?

'We are of those who must live for Samavia – working day and night,' his father had answered; 'denying ourselves, training our bodies and souls, using our brains, learning the things which are best to be done for our people and our country. Even exiles may be Samavian soldiers – I am one, you must be one."

'A story of family, and travel and adventure, filled with bravery and wonder and love. It is a classic story from a classic writer and one full of hidden treasures.'

– Matt Haig,
author of *Shadow Forest*

puck of pook's hill
by rudyard kipling

£7.99 • ISBN 9781843915027
foreword by marcus sedgwick

Una and Dan get the shock of their lives as their play acting summons forth a real-life elf. Enchanted by the tales he tells them, they beg to hear more but Puck can go even further, he can show them...

'You've broken the Hills — you've broken the Hills! It hasn't happened in a thousand years... Unluckily the Hills are empty now, and all the People of the Hills are gone. I'm the only one left. I'm Puck, the oldest Old Thing in England, very much at your service if — if you care to have anything to do with me...'

'It's the stuff of the imagination of anyone who ever lay on an English hilltop on a lazy summer Sunday and wondered about the history of the landscape around them — what do these strange names of the villages and hills around us mean? Why do we feel there must be hidden things in the forest and hedgerows around us?'
— Marcus Sedgwick,
author of *The Raven Mysteries*

the prince and the pauper
by mark twain

£7.99 • ISBN 9781843915034
foreword by jeanne willis

Edward and Tom might look absolutely identical, but their lives couldn't be more different. Edward is a prince while his lookalike, Tom, is a pauper. So when the boys switch places there is no telling what might happen...

In the ancient city of London...a boy was born to a poor family of the name of Canty, who did not want him. On the same day another English child was born to a rich family of the name of Tudor, who did want him. All England wanted him too.

'It is easy to see why this book is still in print – it's as relevant today as it's always been... Long live the king of the Great American Novel.'

— Jeanne Willis,
author of *Who's in the Loo?*